PLAN B

A NOVEL BY

Chester Himes

MIDDLEBURY COLLEGE LIBRARY

EDITED, WITH AN INTRODUCTION, BY

MICHEL   FABRE

& ROBERT E. SKINNER

UNIVERSITY PRESS OF MISSISSIPPI   JACKSON

The editors wish to thank Mr. Lester Sullivan, Archivist, and Mr. Raymond O. Berthelot, Archival Associate, of the Xavier University Department of Archives and Special Collections, for their help in proofreading the drafts of the manuscripts.

Plan B copyright © 1993 by Lesley Himes
Introduction copyright © 1993 by University Press of Mississippi
All rights reserved

Manufactured in the United States of America

96 95 94 93   4 3 2 1

The paper in this book meets the guidelines for permanence and durability of the Committee on Production Guidelines for Book Longevity of the Council on Library Resources.

Library of Congress Cataloging-in-Publication Data

Himes, Chester B., 1909-1984
    Plan B / by Chester Himes ; edited and intro-
    duced by Michel Fabre & Robert E. Skinner.
        p. cm.
    ISBN 0-87805-645-9
    1. Afro-American men—Fiction. 2. Racism—
United States—Fiction. I. Fabre, Michel.
II. Skinner, Robert E., 1948-   . III. Title.
PS3515.I713P58 1993
813'.54—dc20   93-13939
                                    CIP

British Library Cataloging-in-Publication data available

Designed by John A. Langston

INTRODUCTION

There is a particular purgatory of esteem reserved for those American artists who have been lionized in Europe while enduring neglect at home. . . . For both the voluntary exiles and for those who labored in obscurity at home, the final irony of their relative success abroad was that it seemed to delay their recognition in the United States even further.

Thus writes Luc Sante, in "An American Abroad" (*New York Review of Books,* January 16, 1992, 8–12), an article that seems to signal Chester Himes's own emergence from this purgatory, at a time when most of his books have finally been reprinted in English-language editions.

Indeed, the story of Himes's literary career overflows with irony. After his complex, realistic novels of race relations met with only moderate success in the United States, he moved to France where he lived in comparative poverty, if not in obscurity. That is, until Marcel Duhamel, the editor of Editions Gallimard's *Série Noire* detective paperbacks, persuaded him to try his hand at a crime novel set in Harlem. The result, *For Love of Imabelle,* was hailed as a masterpiece by such literary giants as Jean Cocteau and Jean Giono. It achieved the distinction of being awarded the *Grand Prix de la littérature policiere* for 1958—the first time the prestigious prize was awarded to a non-French author.

Chester Himes went on to produce no less than eight other *Série Noire* thrillers in the decade that followed and enjoyed the pleasure (and perhaps the irony, too) of seeing the final entry in the series, *Blind Man with a Pistol,* published in Gallimard's *Série Blanche.* In France, of course, these series titles have nothing at all to do with race. "Roman noir" means "detective novel" in French, a fact that accounted for the black covers of that particular series. The white covers that Gallimard used for its prestigious *Du monde entier* series were reserved for *belles-lettres* from all over the world.

Most of Himes's thrillers, which he preferred to call "domestic" rather than detective novels, were set exclusively in Harlem, with the action shifting from back alley junkyard to Sugar Hill high-rise, from barroom to poolroom, and from church to brothel. They were soon hailed as a "Harlem human comedy" by French reviewers who compared them favorably to Balzac's *comédie humaine*.

All but one featured Coffin Ed Johnson and Grave Digger Jones, a pair of tough, uncompromising black police detectives. Unlike many such characters, Coffin Ed and Grave Digger were complex personalities who daily faced the paradox of serving the white man's law while attempting to provide a modicum of justice for a race that the law continually excluded or victimized. Their dialogue often reflects the bitter irony of their lot and Himes continually uses their voices to denounce racial injustice and the American system that makes it possible.

As the series proceeded, Himes's imagination moved from suckers cheated by "stings," "blow jobs," and con games to multi-million dollar drug traffic; from run-of-the-mill street crime to random psychopathic violence; from the everyday socio-economic woes of the black man in the street to the larger social and political issues that affected, and divided, a nation. *Run Man Run* (first published in French in 1959) features a murderous white police detective as its villain. *The Heat's On* (1961) makes grim sport of the heroin trade. *Cotton Comes to Harlem* (1964) includes a sometimes-comical recasting of Marcus Garvey's Back to Africa movement.

As time went on, Himes's vision broadened to include his disgust for religious leaders who enriched themselves through charlatanry. His increasingly apocalyptic view of racial confrontation artfully illustrated the way the "We Shall Overcome" chants of peaceful civil rights advocates gave way to the Black Power slogans and Black Muslim disquisitions in the years that followed the "burning summers" of 1964–1965.

By 1967, Himes seemed to have forgotten his earlier misgivings about involving himself in what he had once considered an illegitimate literary genre. His critical and commercial success in Europe so thoroughly convinced him of the value of this new phase of his career that he came increasingly to believe that the Harlem Domestic Series might well be his greatest and most enduring contribution to world literature.

By then, he was living well, if not luxuriously. He could even, at long last, contemplate the purchase of a house, although he was disappointed that he still could not afford to live in his favorite area, the French Riviera. After months of fruitless searching for a place in Spain, a place where he believed he would like to live, Himes seemed genuinely pleased when he finally wrote to Roslyn Targ, his literary agent, on December 17, 1968, that he had bought a couple of lots in a development called Pla del Mar, down on the tip of the coast jutting out of picturesque Cabo de la Nao, near the town of Javea in the province of Alicante. "We hope to build our little Spanish house," he added.

That same month, Himes and his wife, Lesley, took up temporary residence in an old palace on Duque de Zaragoza Street in the city of Alicante. Here, Himes was able to write again. A list of unpublished works compiled by his agent around that time included "Hurt White Women," a 446-page narrative that was an early stage of his first volume of autobiography; "The Lunatic Fringe," an all-white murder mystery set in Mallorca that he had been unable to complete for years; and "Blow, Gabriel, Blow," a short movie script about religious con games in Harlem that he had tried vainly to sell.

He wrote to John A. Williams around that same time that "I have now commenced on the wildest and most defiant of my Harlem series, which will wind it up and kill one of my two detectives." The novel may have originated in a short story called "Tang," that was reportedly completed in 1967. Shortly thereafter, he decided to call the new book "Plan B."

Himes began writing it in Alicante while he was designing the plans for his new house. Four months later, he described the book as "the most violent story I have ever attempted, about an *organized* black rebellion which is extremely bloody and violent, as any such rebellion must be." As was usual for him when he was writing, he forged ahead with the narrative without making much of a draft and without having much of an outline, with the possible exception of a synopsis of the book's concluding chapters.

Not too much later, he noted that he had lost his sense of where the book was going. "Anyway, I'm not near finished with it—and then on the other hand it might never be published" (letter to John A. Williams, April 15, 1969). He did, however, complete at least enough of the novel to derive from it a long short story that he called "The Birth of Chitterlings, Inc." The story was to have been part of a never-published collection of short stories that was to have been entitled *Black on White*. He wrote in the foreword to the collection that he had written the story while "contemplating how blacks could get guns into the U. S. to stage a revolution." Meanwhile, what were apparently two other sections of "Plan B," a short story called "Tang" and another called "Celebration" saw publication in *Black on Black*, a collection of stories and essays that was issued in 1972.

Plan B may well have been supplanted in favor of *Blind Man with a Pistol*, a subsequent novel that tackled the same social and political issues. From the end of August 1969 until near the end of a very rainy November when he returned to Paris suffering from hypertension, Chester Himes stayed in Holland with Lesley. He wanted to visit his Dutch agent and spend the summer there after their Paris sublet expired. In a luxurious house in Blaricum, he and Lesley enjoyed for a time a hitherto unknown degree of comfort.

It was during this stay that they were visited by a younger black expatriate writer named Phil Lomax. One day, Lomax called Chester on "urgent business" and was told to come right away. What Lomax wanted was to plead forgiveness because he had plagarized a section of *Pinktoes* into a barely disguised rewrite that he had sold in the Netherlands. Chester was magnanimous. Not only did he forgive Lomax, but he invited him to stay for lunch, during which he spoke freely and at some length to the young writer. As they swapped stories, Lomax related an anecdote about a blind man with a gun who began shooting at random in the New York subway. Exactly why he had done so was not clear.

Maybe he'd wanted to pretend to himself that he could see, or perhaps he just wanted to feel that he existed for others.

This story found its way into the new thriller Himes was busily working on. He had already completed many sundry episodes, yet without finding the thread between them. At that stage, he decided that absurdity itself should become the unifying theme. He even took the phrase "the blind man with a pistol" as the title for his book, and graciously credited Lomax in a foreword to the published novel. In unpublished notes for his autobiography Himes explained:

> By accident I wrote two words: "the dying man gasped: 'Jesus Baby'," and never finished the sentence, but the dying man had intended to say: "Jesus, Baby, you did not have to kill me." In Holland, I wrote the end of the sentence: "You didn't have to kill me," then took it out because I found another ending: The Blind Man with his pistol. It made a perfect ending for the story because I had launched on to a different kind of story where I could accuse everyone of inhumanity.
>
> Phil Lomax told me a story of the Blind Man with his pistol which was my story of all people: confusion, misunderstanding, confrontation with death at the hands of legality.

Himes added, significantly:

> That was the story of all black people, but I never wrote it. I lost myself in trying to write a successful story about black people: *Plan B*.

If we are to believe Himes, he was still thinking about completing *Plan B* after bringing *Blind Man with a Pistol* to a successful conclusion.

At any rate, in September 1970 Himes sent his agent a new short story called "Pork Chop Paradise" which corresponds to "The Birth of Chitterlings, Inc.," and clearly is a section of the uncompleted novel. In October 1972, he trimmed a story corresponding to an early section in the same novel, deleting its first four sections, and called it "Prediction." This story made its way into the collection, *Black on Black*. He felt confident that this fifth section was enough to make his point without straining credulity (Letter to E. Varkala, October 23, 1972).

The rest of the manuscript remained in a drawer in his little office in Villa Griot, where his failing health allowed him to repair only infrequently now. It lay there until February of 1982, when the Paris-based Editions Lieu Commun asked Michel Fabre to try and secure for them some unpublished material from Himes. A number of his short stories were still unpublished, even in English, because his "Black on White" collection had never appeared in the United States. There were also many stories that had originally appeared in American magazines during the 1930s and 1940s that remained uncollected. From this wealth of material, a volume of short stories in French, entitled *Le Manteau de rêve*, was published in 1982. Always eager to read Himes after the success of his early protest fiction and his later detective novels, French critics and readers alike enthusiastically welcomed the new collection.

At that stage, Michel Fabre discovered the typescript of *Plan B,* a few pages of which Himes had recently torn up and thrown away in a fit of rage. His deteriorating health had handicapped him to such an extent that he could no longer write at all. Along with the typescript, Fabre discovered a synopsis of the final section. Seeing that it was written out in an expanded draft form with elaborate dialogues, Fabre realized that it could serve as a proper conclusion. He therefore worked on establishing a version of the novel, a task that required the excision of a few repetitious episodes and a strict adherence to the corrected version. This work served as the basis for the French translation, published in 1983 by Lieu Commun. To provide the present version, Robert Skinner has carefully edited this text, a process that involved the incorporation of more recently-discovered typed and hand-written revisions that Himes had added to his original draft. In this process, he made every effort to ultimately produce a manuscript that reflected a genuine respect for the author's socio-political intentions and stylistic concerns.

In 1983, Chester Himes painstakingly signed his last piece. In September he had received a circular letter from the *International Herald Tribune,* asking him to renew his long-expired subscription. With Lesley's help, he composed a letter which showed that he still retained his devastating sense of humor. It read in part:

I do not disagree that the *Herald Tribune* is "the only American international daily." What I am annoyed about is the fact that they NEVER, NEVER mentioned my books [during] my years of writing in Europe, even when my last book, *Un Manteau de rêve,* (sic) received enthusiastic reviews from most important French newspapers and literary magazines . . . . I am an American, black and very proud to be both. You have ignored me completely and this is why I borrow my neighbors' papers, FREE, when I feel the need to read your newspaper. Indeed, why pay? . . . . Will you "welcome me into your daily life?" I'm not dead yet and I will have another book out in France in a week or so. It is called *Plan B* . . . . It is an unfinished detective story.

Proud and comforted as he now was by the certainty of the book's publication, Himes did not live to see *Plan B* brought out by Editions Lieu Commun and to see it even more widely and enthusiastically welcomed by French critics and readers than was *Le Manteau de rêve.*

Before trying to analyze the contents and tone of the novel, it may be worthwhile to consider some of the reviews that hailed the French publication of this novel, in order to show not only how seriously it was taken, but also to place Himes's literary reputation in its proper international context.

One French critic, who asserted that Himes would go down in history as the greatest black writer of the century, considered *Plan B* a delirious legacy that explored the implacable hatred existing between black and white. The unnamed critic felt that Himes had benefited greatly from his move into detective fiction because he used the form to skillfully explore deeper concerns. Other reviews insisted that the book was a great pleasure to read, even though Himes's detectives died in an effort to solve an insoluble political issue. It was "vintage Himes, indeed." Many observed that, although Himes had left the book incomplete, the reader need have no reservations about reading it. Admittedly it was a strange book, unbalanced because it started out in the purest *Série Noire* style then ended as a political tract about the American racial problem, but this did not diminish the passion of Himes's prose.

Jean-Pierre Bonicco regarded Himes's description of the ghetto as hyperrealistic and flamboyant, causing his thriller to turn into a novel of manners. The "great American writer of immense talents" was a "literary alchemist" who could transform his bleak story into a kind of literary gold. The reviewer mourned the fact that the deaths of Coffin Ed and Grave Digger spelled the end to the Harlem saga, but he regarded the novel as Himes's bloody farewell to literature and to his legacy of despair ("Le Forum des livres: *Plan B,* par Chester Himes." *Var Matin,* December 18, 1983).

Maurice Decroix characterized *Plan B* as "a picaresque, many-hued novel that Himes wrote in the heyday of the Black Panthers and Black Muslims." He advised readers to rush out to get this book, even if only to read Himes's descriptions of Eighth Avenue in Harlem in the August heat

("Au rayon du polar." *Nord Eclair* October 27, 1983). Writing for the Paris illustrated weekly *VSD,* Jean-Pierre Enard considered "the ultimate novel by one of America's greatest authors," as "strong as a glass of gin, rhythmical as a Charlie Parker solo" ("Livres: *Plan B,* de Chester Himes." *VSD* November 24, 1983, 21).

The well-known Le Monde critic and Himes's regular reviewer, Bernard Géniès, made much of the fact that Himes went on a wholesale killing spree that envelopes even his two detectives. Géniès believed that the story, set against a backdrop reminiscent of the ghetto revolts of the 1960s, must be read in that perspective to be fully appreciated. Had Himes wanted to end his series and take revenge upon his cast of characters, he wondered? His many references to slavery were seen by Géniès as evidence of a "more realistic vision" ("Quand Chester Himes assassine ses héros." *Le Monde,* October 12, 1983, xii).

In a later piece, "Retour à Chester Himes," Géniès apparently had second thoughts. He regretted that Himes never managed to dig beneath the surface of his poverty-stricken Harlèm backdrop in order to become a second Richard Wright. He insisted, though, that Himes's meeting with *Série Noire* editor Marcel Duhamel had enabled him to attain his own identity as a writer (*Le Monde,* November 4, 1983, xiii).

Speaking of Himes's "splendid failure," Stéphane Jousni noted that, at his best, Himes had kept his two black detectives aloof from the race issue. In *Plan B,* a novel transformed into a political and racial tract, the pair took sides in the conflict and were killed. She believed that the book should be read for its memorable, surrealistic descriptions of Harlem life. For Jousni, as for Jean Giono, Himes was a writer superior to Hemingway, Dos Passos, and Fitzgerald ("Un admirable 'raté' de Chester Himes." *La Libre Belgique,* October 13, 1983).

The *Le Matin* critic used the French title of an earlier Himes thriller to characterize *Plan B* as an "Imbroglio negro." He stressed that the career of protagonist Tomsson Black ran parallel to an apocalyptic increase in violence and an ensuing moral dilemma. "It would not be fitting," he wrote, "to call such gutsy writing baroque." For him, the novel stood as "both a testament to Himes's talent and the apotheosis of his career" (*Le Matin,* October 27, 1983, 26).

In the left-wing *La Marseilluise,* Françoise Poignant noted that after a humorous opening, Himes's angriest, blackest novel becomes a nightmare that deteriorates into a bloodbath. She wondered if Himes had been unable to find a proper conclusion to this impasse or if he had become so ill that he could no longer write ("*Plan B:* un livre plein de dureur et de bruit." November 27, 1983, 6).

Fréderic Vitoux's review, "Au bout de la nuit: *Plan B* par Chester Himes," at once established a link with Louis-Ferdinand Céline's classic narrative of marginality, *Voyage au bout de la nuit.* Vitoux called *Plan B* a book "as black as ink, as blood, as stupidity, as memory, as hatred, as slavery, as America in 1969 . . . . Himes takes the reader to hell with an almost suicidal relish, then dazzles us with his descriptions of crime, injustice, and rebellion in Harlem." Vitoux felt that the book was bound to remain unfinished because no logical conclusion could really be derived from such large-scale racial strife. He noted wryly that trips to the end of the world have no real conclusion (*Nouvel Observateur,* November 11, 1983).

Christiane Falgayrettes chose to set the book against a wider background. She stated that Himes preferred scorn and humor to the violence and open hatred evidenced in Wright's and Baldwin's works. She also compared Himes favorably with Ellison, concluding that Himes preferred to act upon the guilty conscience of his white readership (*La Montagne,* July 29, 1984, 6).

Cameroonian academic Ambroise Kom, himself the author of a detailed study of Himes's novels, found that *Plan B* combined the absurdity of *For Love of Imabelle,* the grim overtones of *Blind Man with a Pistol,* and the succulent flavor of *Pinktoes.* Kom expressed the view that the book left unanswered many questions about Himes's own vision of the United States ("Chester Himes *Plan B.*" *Notre Librairie,* No. 77, November–December 1984, 125–126).

A few reactions were intensely political. In *Révolution,* Michael Naudy, undoubtedly thinking of Marx and Engels, claimed that Himes was the legitimate heir to the nineteenth-century revolutionary theoreticians of Central Europe. He said that Himes created such a vast human comedy that he should rightfully be called "a dark Balzac" ("Le fils légitime." *Révolution,* November 28, 1984, 39).

In another left-wing publication, *Liberté,* Françoise Poignant also dealt with a new reprint of *The Big Gold Dream* in her review of *Plan B.* She wondered if there was any solution to America's race problem and suggested that Himes's way of coping with it was to write in a picaresque style that resorted to caricature and surrealism. *The Big Gold Dream,* she said, was a successful story filled with non-stop humor. *Plan B,* on the other hand, was a nightmarish description of race hatred that offered overwhelming fury and desperation but proposed no solution ("Harlem au bout de la nuit." *Liberté,* December 4, 1984).

When Chester Himes died in mid-November of 1984, the entire French press paid him tribute. Obituaries surveyed his career as a convict, writer, and expatriate. They invariably stressed the importance of his detective fiction and of his lively picture of Harlem. Laudatory comments about Himes's talent by younger French detective writers such as Michel Lebrun, Pierre Siniac, and Patrick Manchette were often quoted. Since *Plan B* was just out, many obituaries mentioned it at length.

The critic for the left-wing daily, *La Marseillaise,* noted that Himes had brought nobility to detective fiction by using it to protest America's racist society. *Blind Man with a Pistol* was praised as a "splendid metaphor" and *Plan B* was described as "an apocalyptic struggle." The writer concluded that Himes's tough, authentic novels, all of which were firmly anchored in reality, would leave a lasting imprint on American literature (November 14, 1984).

While readers can't fail to experience revulsion at some aspects of the book, they should be favorably struck by the structure and style. It soon becomes clear that the non-linear construction with its wildly alternating, and apparently unrelated plots, recalls Faulkner's work in *The Wild Palms*. As is true in Faulkner's work, the twin story lines actually intensify the suspense.

It is interesting to realize that a book that made such an impact on European audiences has yet to be seen by American readers. For years, scholars and fans of Chester Himes's Harlem Domestic Series, piqued by Himes's own remarks, have discussed the possible existence of a "lost" entry in the series, one that included the tragic deaths of one or both of Himes's two heroes, Coffin Ed Johnson and Grave Digger Jones. The rumors even inspired a novel by African writer Njami Simon, published as *Cercueil et Cie* (Paris: Editions Lieu Commun, 1985) in France and later in the United States as *Coffin and Company* (Berkeley, California: Black Lizard Books, 1987).

During the time he was writing *Plan B,* Himes alluded to his work on it in several interviews, most notably the one conducted by John A. Williams that was published in *Amistad 1* (New York: Random House, 1970). Himes invariably discussed the plot to this book in context with his deep discouragement with the lack of improvement in race relations in the United States.

Over a long period of years he had come to believe that the only way blacks could truly achieve equality in America was through some kind of violent revolutionary behavior. Writing in 1944, Himes suggested that progress can only be brought about by revolution, that revolutions can only be started by incidents, and that incidents can only be created by martyrs. Although his process seems to be a forerunner of Dr. Martin Luther King's method of non-violent change, Himes saw things in the opposite light. He stated that Negro martyrs were needed to "create the incident which will mobilize the forces of justice and carry us forward from the pivot of change to a way of existence wherein everyone is free." ("Negro Martyrs Are Needed." *The Crisis,* 51, May 1944, 174).

By the time of his *Amistad* interview, Himes was preaching what would have been considered sedition in an earlier time. As he told Williams, "I can see what a black revolution would be like . . . . First of all, in order for a revolution to be effective, one of the things that it has to be, is violent, it has to be massively violent; it has to be as violent as the war in Viet Nam . . . . In any form of uprising, the major objective is to kill as many people as you can, by whatever means you can kill them, because the very fact of killing them and killing them in sufficient numbers is supposed to help you gain your objectives."

Himes's view of revolution was one in which no prisoners were taken. He went on to say that "the black people kill as many of the people of the white community as they can kill. That means children, women, grown men, industrialists, street sweepers or whatever they are, as long as they're white. And this is the fact that gains its objective—there's no discussion—no point in doing anything else, and no reason to give it any thought." (p.45) One cannot help but be reminded of Williams's own *The Man Who Cried I Am* (Boston: Little Brown, 1967), but in reverse. Himes was a great admirer of Williams's fiction and it is possible that he may have been trying to create an equivalent of his friend's "King Alfred Plan" to destroy the black race.

Whatever his intention, it is clear that Himes saw the black man as a powerful, indomitable presence who could actually bring down the American nation through calculated, suicidal acts of violence, and he attempted to suggest just how this could be done in ways that were so brutal, so graphic, so disgusting, that even at the time he was writing it he said "I don't know what the American publishers will do about this book. But one thing I do know . . . they will hesitate, and it will cause them a great amount of revulsion, because the scenes that I have described will be revolting scenes." (p.47) Himes realized the power of such writing, but he felt that the writing of violence was natural to the American writer. As he said to Williams, "American violence is public life, it's a public way of life . . ." (p.49)

An important portion of *Plan B* details an unprovoked attack by a resolute, virile, black martyr who ambushes a parade of policemen with an automatic rifle. Eventually, when conventional methods of subduing him fail, a tank is brought in to actually demolish the building in which he is hiding. This counter-attack is so extreme and so destructive that the stock market falls and the United States begins to disappear as a nation.

"The Birth of Chitterlings, Inc." sequence is part picaresque tale and partly the adventures of a black master criminal named Tomsson Black. As a prelude, Himes takes the reader far back into American history, to the Alabama swamps of the late 1850s. A rather lengthy digression about the travails of the degenerate Harrison family sets the stage for the development of "piquant" chitterlings from razorback hogs fed on a diet of sweet potatoes. This is followed by the complete family tree of the black Lincoln family, to whom Himes introduces us in the pre-Civil War South. Himes describes in detail the adventures of each generation of Lincolns until we finally meet George Washington Lincoln, who later takes the name Tomsson Black, a name originally given to him in insult, but which he later adopts because it emphasizes his "blackness."

Throughout this story, Himes provides us with a rather insistent view that white Southerners are sexually degenerate. His purpose in doing so is not clear, but the space he allots to the presumption makes it impossible to ignore.

Himes also uses the character of Tomsson Black to express his oft-stated belief that black sexuality was irresistible to whites, and particularly to white women.

Tomsson Black becomes Himes's mouthpiece for much of the course of the story. Although we discover that Black has deliberately travelled to every communist country hostile to the United States, consorted with the leaders, and learned as much as he could about the violent and clandestine overthrow of governments, Black seems initially to be a rather benign character. His troubles, and his change in personality, come about after he is driven to rape Barbara Goodfeller, a rich and depraved white socialite.

Himes's personal attraction to white women is well known, so it is possible to see parts of him in the character of Tomsson Black. This is particularly evident in Black's mingled desire for and disgust with interracial sex and in his belief that black skin brings out the depraved nature inherent in white women. These ideologies will be familiar to anyone who has read *If He Hollers Let Him Go* and *The Primitive*. As was true for the protagonists of those earlier books, Black recognizes that white women are a trap that he cannot avoid falling into. Neither can he keep from allowing his disgust for white women to degenerate into violence. After the rape and beating of Barbara Goodfeller, Black rages to her effete and ineffectual husband "There's nothing you can do with a slut like this but beat her. Not if you're trapped. Not if you're black."

After his imprisonment for the rape (which happens, appropriately enough, in Alabama), Black becomes a brooding presence and gradually transforms into a kind of archfiend/master criminal in the vein of Professor Moriarity or Phantomas. All of his energies go into concocting the public personae of black philanthropist and friend to the white community while secretly plotting the violent overthrow of American society. In this we can see the seeds of Dr. Moore, who tells an assistant "what I need is a dead man" in order to have a more productive riot, and the Prophet Ham, a half-mad preacher who has organized his religious cult for the purpose of ramming the black Jesus down the white man's throat. Each of these characters makes an effective, chilling appearance in Himes's book, *Blind Man with a Pistol,* published in 1969.

How Coffin Ed and Grave Digger, Himes's two indomitable detectives, ended up in *Plan B* is rather puzzling. From the very beginning, Himes seems to have had it in mind to write a story in which not even they could conquer the power of racism. What is particularly interesting about their all-too-brief place in the story is the fact that it is Grave Digger, always the more sensible and thoughtful of the pair, who loses his temper and starts the ball rolling. Normally articulate and rational, Grave Digger's rise to anger and subsequent execution of T-bone Smith are as out of character as his vague statement that the murdered prostitute, Tang, reminds him of his mother.

Although he has traditionally been the most ideologically "black" member of the detective team, Digger's decision, late in the novel, to throw in his lot with Tomsson Black rather than bring him to justice, seems unnatural and is, perhaps as Himes intended, a surprise. That he would subsequently murder Coffin Ed after each has risked his life for the other in so many other adventures, is also a surprise, and an unpleasant one at that.

Although we will never know just what Himes intended, it seems clear in retrospect that he had come to disbelieve the possibility of simple justice for American black people, just as he had become certain of the necessity of organized and armed black revolution to change the American system. In *Blind Man with a Pistol,* he artfully amplifies these beliefs in an alternative scenario where his normally unbeatable heroes are stopped in their tracks by forces so sinister, so deeply imbedded, that they cannot even see them. Himes's reduction of their status from knights-errant to rat exterminators at the conclusion of *Blind Man* is a far more powerful comment on the defeat of justice than his symbolic murder of them in the final existing scene of *Plan B.*

Plan B thus remains an incandescent parable of racial madness as well as a retrospective of American racial history. The book begins as a thriller, then races toward a horrible climax. One might characterize it as a black *Apocalypse Now,* and although things are quieter now than they were in the 1960s, Himes's vision still strikes the reader's heart and reminds one of the angry unrest that still lies beneath the exterior of American society. Here, his fundamental pessimism reaches a paroxistic dimension in which sexuality can only be bestial, violence ruthless, and racism absolute.

Concluding the adventures of Coffin Ed and Grave Digger with a bang, *Plan B* brims over with extreme situations and an occasional lewdness that seems at times to parody the Southern Gothic tradition of Erskine Caldwell and William Faulkner. Indeed, Himes must have thought of the antebellum mirage of Sutpen's acres and the decadent intrigues of the Compton family while concocting the genealogies of his protagonists in ways that sometimes seem to mock *Gone with the Wind*. We know that his reverence for the author of *Sanctuary* was deep and lasting, and that he loved the irreverent, unlikely episodes of *The Reivers,* which cheered him up while he was in New York Presbyterian Hospital undergoing tests after his stroke in April of 1964. Still, whatever humor there may be in Tomsson Black's memories of his days in the South, it is thickly overlaid with cold, black rage. Life in Himes's South is a negative image of Faulkner's.

While verisimilitude is often strained to the utmost, there is yet a realistic strain, at times reminiscent of the spare, matter-of-fact personal histories or explanatory genealogies of the five black protagonists of Himes's *A Case of Rape*. It also takes little time to discover that Tomsson's coming of age after the killing of his father by an angry white and the hero's subsequent years in jail only repeat the tragic destiny of many a real black family—whether we think of the killing of Richard Wright's Uncle Hoskins by a jealous West Helena, Arkansas, competitor, or the lynching of Malcolm X's father. Indeed, the figure of Malcolm X looms large in this novel, although it does so symbolically, at second remove. Clearly, though, the growth in political awareness of the intransigent Black Muslim leader (whom Himes had briefly befriended while shooting a documentary in Harlem, and who had made it a point to climb ten flights of stairs in order to talk to Himes in his Latin Quarter apartment) is very much present in Tomsson Black's itinerary.

Like much of Himes's writing, *Plan B* has its autobiographical touch. Those familiar with Himes's own family story and the records that his literary-minded mother, Estelle Bomar, kept of her own ancestry and childhood in "Old Lick Log," will be able to relate more than one detail of Tomsson Black's parentage, or Alabama life, to Himes's background and to his own early memories at Port Gibson or at Alcorn State College.

Perhaps more than anything else, *Plan B* is a symbolic answer to the questions posed by the Black Power movement. One must observe that Himes did not believe in violence as a solution to anything—that is to say that he did not believe in the power of *unorganized* violence. This is thought to be the reason why Himes left this novel unfinished, that he may have reached an ideological impasse.

An analysis of the function of Coffin Ed and Grave Digger in his Harlem Domestic novels, suggests that, while they fought black crime and white prejudice, they were also symbols of integration. In this novel, Himes goes so far as to kill his duo, after one of them has joined the ranks of radical Black nationalism. This amounts to literary suicide and one can well understand why Himes became stalled and could not carry the book through to publication during the early 1970s.

The deaths of Himes's heroes close out a novel filled with racy episodes and bizarre plot twists and which culminates in a civil war, replete with manhunts and surrealistic escalations of violence. Much of Himes's genius lies in his fleshy descriptions of teeming ghetto life, descriptions that recall the paintings of Bosch or the French illustrator, Dubout. Through his peculiar brand of absurd humor, Himes is able to explore America's worst racial fears without directly confronting them.

Although the reader may be appalled by the bloody atrocities and pervasive conflict in *Plan* B, he may still retain an admiration for Himes's skill as a social analyst. His narrative adventure is, at the same time, an opportunity for him to examine the minds of both blacks and whites under the stress of racial antagonism. This lucid, bitter indictment of both races may leave the reader uneasy, but it is impossible to ignore Himes's virtuosity in his imaginative representation of a racist America. His story begins with the roots of racial evil during the slavery era, then swells into a picture of apocalyptic violence and interracial slaughter during the riots of the 1960s, a period when the prevailing contact between blacks and whites was characterized by mistrust and violence.

Himes's logic and clear-sightedness are frightening, and the result is an angry, violent story. In *Plan B*, Himes creates an insistent image of the black man as a sexual symbol, then reflects it back into white consciousness. This brooding, virile image turns against the white American world the same weapons that were fashioned to subjugate his people. Given such circumstances, Himes's black detectives can no longer represent law and order, even according to their unorthodox interpretation of it. They are foreordained to disappear in a cataclysmic explosion of racial violence.

Plan B is a hard book that leaves the reader with a flinty taste in his mouth. It is "political" fiction, as well as a preamble to the subtler and ultimately more amusing picture of black and white ways of thinking that Himes ultimately achieved in *Blind Man with a Pistol*. Apart from the nonstop action and titillating dialogue, *Plan B* remains an excellent example of the peculiar blend of surrealism and humor that Himes used to withstand the torments that he must have felt from a lifetime of facing the injustice of American racial policies.

Michel Fabre

Robert E. Skinner

PLAN B

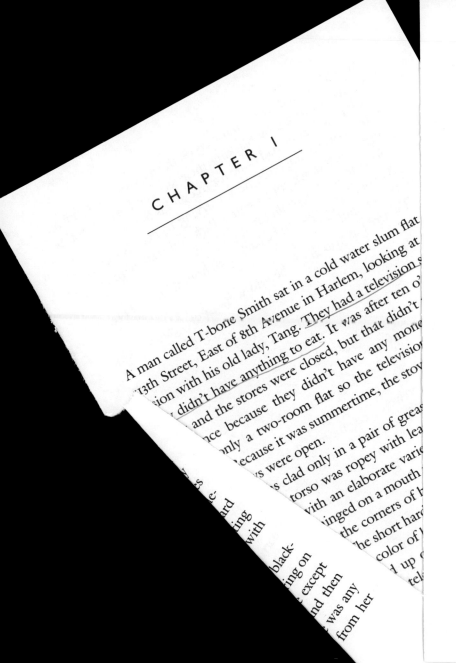

two blackfaced white minstrels on the television screen who earned a fortune by blacking their faces and acting just as foolish as T-bone had done for free all his life.

In between laughing, he was trying to get his old lady, Tang, to go down into Central Park and trick with some white man so they could eat.

"Go on, baby, you can be back in an hour with 'nuff bread so we can scoff."

"I'se tired as you are," she said with an evil glance. "Go sell yo' own ass to whitey, you luvs him so much."

She had once been a beautiful jet-black woman with softly rounded features in a broad flat face and a figure to evoke instant visions of writhing sexuality and black ecstasy.

But both her face and figure had been corroded by vice and hunger, and now she was just a lean, angular crone with burnt red hair and flat black features that looked like they had been molded by a stamping machine. Only her eyes looked alive: they were red, mean, disillusioned and defiant. She was clad in a soiled faded green mother hubbard, and her big buniony feet trod restlessly about the rotten kitchen linoleum. The tops of her feet were covered wrinkled black skin streaked with white dirt.

Suddenly, above the sound of the gibbering of the face white minstrels, they heard an impatient hammering the door. They couldn't imagine anyone it could be the police. They looked sharply at one another they looked quickly about the room to see if there incriminating evidence in sight, although, aside

PLAN B

CHAPTER 1

A man called T-bone Smith sat in a cold water slum flat on 113th Street, East of 8th Avenue in Harlem, looking at television with his old lady, Tang. They had a television set but they didn't have anything to eat. It was after ten o'clock at night and the stores were closed, but that didn't make any difference because they didn't have any money, anyway. It was only a two-room flat so the television was in the kitchen. Because it was summertime, the stove was cold and the windows were open.

T-bone was clad only in a pair of greasy black pants and his bare black torso was ropey with lean hard muscles and was decorated with an elaborate variety of scars. His long narrow face was hinged on a mouth with lips the size of automobile tires and the corners of his sloe-shaped eyes were sticky with mucus. The short hard burrs on his watermelon-shaped head were the color of half-burnt ashes. He had his bare black feet propped up on the kitchen table with the white soles toward the television screen. He was white-mouthed from hunger but was laughing like an idiot at two blackfaced white minstrels on the television screen who earned a fortune by blacking their faces and acting just as foolish as T-bone had done for free all his life.

In between laughing, he was trying to get his old lady, Tang, to go down into Central Park and trick with some white man so they could eat.

"Go on, baby, you can be back in an hour with 'nuff bread so we can scoff."

"I'se tired as you are," she said with an evil glance. "Go sell yo' own ass to whitey, you luvs him so much."

She had once been a beautiful jet-black woman with softly rounded features in a broad flat face and a figure to evoke instant visions of writhing sexuality and black ecstasy. But both her face and figure had been corroded by vice and hunger, and now she was just a lean, angular crone with burnt red hair and flat black features that looked like they had been molded by a stamping machine. Only her eyes looked alive: they were red, mean, disillusioned and defiant. She was clad in a soiled faded green mother hubbard and her big buniony feet trod restlessly about the rotting kitchen linoleum. The tops of her feet were covered with wrinkled black skin streaked with white dirt.

Suddenly, above the sound of the gibbering of the black-face white minstrels, they heard an impatient hammering on the door. They couldn't imagine anyone it could be except the police. They looked sharply at one another and then they looked quickly about the room to see if there was any incriminating evidence in sight, although, aside from her hustling in the area encircling the lagoon, neither of them had committed any crime recently enough to interest the police. She stuck her bare feet into some old felt slippers and quickly rubbed red lipstick over her rusty lips and he got up and shambled across the floor in his bare feet and opened the door.

A young, uniformed black messenger with smooth skin and bright, intelligent eyes asked, "Mister Smith?"

"Dass me," T-bone admitted.

The messenger extended a long cardboard box wrapped in gilt paper and tied with red ribbon. Conspicuous on the gilt wrapping paper was the green and white label of a florist, decorated with pink and yellow flowers, and in the place for the name and address were the typed words: "Mr. T. Smith, West 113th Street, 4th floor." The messenger placed the box directly into T-bone's outstretched hands and before releasing it, waited until T-bone had a firm grip.

"Flowers for you, sir," he trilled.

T-bone was so startled by this bit of information he almost let go of the box, but the messenger was already hurtling down the stairs, and in any case, T-bone was too slow-witted to do more than stare. He simply stood there, holding the box in his out-stretched hands, his mouth hanging open, not a thought in his head; he just looked stupid and stunned.

But Tang's thoughts were churning suspiciously behind her red eyes.

"Who sending you flowers, black and ugly as you is?" she

demanded from across the room. She really meant it: *who would be sending him flowers, black and ugly as he was, not to mention lazy, and so arrogant in bed he acted like his dick was made of solid uranium.* Still, he was her man, simple-minded or not, and it made her jealous for him to get flowers, other than for his funeral.

"Dese ain't flowers," he said, sounding just as suspicious as she had. "Lessen they be flowers of lead."

"Maybe it's some scoff from the government's thing for the poor folks," she surmised hopefully.

"Not unless it's pigiron knuckes."

She went over beside him and gingerly fingered the white-wrapped box. "It's got your name on it," she said. "And your address. What would anybody be sending to your name and address?"

"We gonna soon see," he said, and stepped across the room to lay the box atop the table. It made a clunking sound. Meanwhile, the two blackfaced white comedians danced merrily on the television screen until interrupted by a beautiful blonde reading a commercial for *Nucreme,* a product that made dirty skin so fresh and white.

She stood back and watched him break the ribbon and tear off the white wrapping paper. She was practically holding her breath when he opened the gray cardboard carton, but he was too unimaginative to have any thoughts about it one way or another. If God had sent him down a trunk full of gold bricks from heaven, he would have wondered who expected him to brick up some holes in a wall that wasn't his. NEGATIVE VIEW OF BLACKNESS CONTROLLED BY WHITES

Inside the cardboard box they saw a long object wrapped in brown oiled paper and packed in paper excelsior, the way they had seen machine tools packed when they had worked in a shipyard in Newark before she had listened to his sweet talk and had come to Harlem to be his whore. GENDER She couldn't imagine anybody sending him a machine tool unless he had been engaged in activities which she didn't know anything about. Which wasn't likely, she thought, as long as she made enough to feed him. He just stared at it stupidly, wondering why anybody would send him something which looked like something he couldn't use even if he wanted to use it.

"Pick it up," she said sharply. "It ain't gonna bite you."

"I ain't scared of nuttin' bitin' me," he said, fearlessly lifting the object from its bed of excelsior. "It ain't heavy as I thought," he said stupidly, although he had given no indication of what he had thought.

She saw a white sheet of instructions underneath the object. Quickly she snatched it up.

"Wuss dat?" he asked with the quick, defensive suspicion of one who can't read.

She knew he couldn't read and a feminine compulsion to needle him because he had been sent something that he couldn't understand inspired her to say, "Writing! That's what."

"What's it say?" he demanded, panic-stricken.

PLAN B

7

She read the printed words to herself: *WARNING!! DO NOT INFORM POLICE!!! LEARN YOUR WEAPON AND WAIT FOR INSTRUCTIONS!!! REPEAT!!! LEARN YOUR WEAPON AND WAIT FOR INSTRUCTIONS!!! WARNING!!! DO NOT INFORM POLICE!!! FREEDOM IS NEAR!!!*

Then she read them aloud. They so alarmed him that sweat broke out over his face; his eyes stretched until they were completely round. Frantically he began tearing the oiled wrapping paper from the object in his hand. The dull blue gleam of an automatic rifle came into sight. She gasped. She had never seen a rifle that looked as dangerous as this. But he had seen and handled such a rifle when he had served in the army during the Korean War.

"Iss a M14," he said. "Iss an army gun."

He was terrified. His skin dried and turned dark gray.

"I done served my time," he went on, and then realizing how stupid that sounded, he added, "Efen iss stolen I don't want it. Wuss anybody wanna send me a stolen gun for?"

Her red eyes blazed in a face contorted by excitement. "It's the uprising, nigger!" she cried. "We gonna be free!"

"Uprising?" He shied away from the word as though it were a vicious dog. "Free?" He jumped as thought he had been bitten by a rattlesnake. "Ise already free. All someone wants to do is get my ass in jail 'cause I'm free." He held the rifle as though it were a bomb which might go off in his hand.

She looked at the gun with awe and admiration. "That'll

chop a white policeman two ways, sides and flat. That'll blow the shit out of whitey's asshole."

"Wut?" He put the gun down onto the table and pushed it away from him. "Shoot a white police? Someun 'spects me tuh shoot de white police?"

"Why not? You wanna uprise, don't you?"

"Uprise? Whore, is you crazy? Uprise where?"

"Uprise here, nigger. Is you that stupid? Here we is and here we is gonna uprise."

"Not me! I ain't gonna get my ass blown off waving that thing around. We had them things in Korea and them Koreans still kilt us niggers like flies."

"You got shit in your blood," she said contemptuously. "Let me feel that thing."

She picked the rifle up from the table and held it as though she were shooting an invasion of cops. "Baby," she said directly to the gun. "You and me can make it, baby."

"Wuss de matter wid you? You crazy?" he shouted.

"Put that thing down. I'm gonna go tell de man fo' we gets both our ass in jail."

"You going to tell whitey?" she asked in surprise. "You gonna run tell the man 'bout this secret that'll make you free?"

"Shut yo' mouth, whore, I'se doin' it much for you as I is for me."

At first she didn't take him too seriously. "For me, nigger? You think I wanna sell my pussy to whitey all my life?" But with the gun in her hand, the question was rhetorical. She kept shooting at imaginary whiteys about the room, thinking she could go hunting and kill her a whitey or two. Hell, give her enough time and bullets she could kill them all.

But her words had made him frown disapprovingly.

"You wanna stop being a whore, whore?" he asked in amazement. "Hell, whore, we gotta live."

"You call this living?" She drew the gun tight to her breast as though it were a lover. "This is the only thing that made me feel alive since I met you."

He looked outraged. "You been lissening to that Black Power shit, them Black Panthers 'n that shit," he accused. "Ain' I always done what's best?"

"Yeah, put me on the block to sell my black pussy to poor white trash."

"I ain' gonna argy wid you," he said in exasperation. "I'se goan 'n get de cops 'fore we both winds up daid."

Slowly and deliberately, she aimed the gun at him. "You call whitey and I'll waste you," she threatened.

He was moving toward the door but the sound of her voice stopped him. He turned about and looked at her. It was more the sight of her than the meaning of her words which made him hesitate. He wasn't a man to dare anyone and she looked as though she would blow him away. But he knew she was a tenderhearted woman and wouldn't hurt him as long as he didn't cross her, so he decided to kid her along until he could grab the gun, then he'd whip her ass. With this in mind he began shuffling around the table in her direction, white teeth showing in a false grin, eyes half-closed like a forgiving lover.

"Baby, I were jes playin—"

"Maybe you is but I ain't," she warned him.

"I wasn't gonna call the cops, I was jes gonna see if the door is locked."

"You see and you won't know it."

She talkin' too much, he thought, shuffling closer. "Baby, leeme show you how to work that thing."

"What's there to do?" she challenged, dropping her gaze to the trigger guard.

Suddenly he grabbed. She pulled the trigger. Nothing happened. Both became frozen in shock. It had never occurred to either of them that the gun was not loaded.

T-bone was the first to react. He burst out laughing. "Haw-haw-haw."

"Woudn't have been so funny if this thing had been loaded," she said sourly.

His face contorted from a delayed reaction of rage. It was as though a hole in his emotions left by the dissipation of his fear had filled up with fury. He whipped out a spring blade knife. "I teach you, whore," he raved. "You try to kill me."

She looked from the knife to his face and said stoically, "I shoulda known, you are whitey's slave; you'll never be free."

"Free of you," he shouted and began slashing at her.

She tried to protect herself with the rifle but shortly he

had cut it out of her grasp. She backed around the table trying to keep away from the slashing blade. But soon the blade began reaching her flesh, the floor became covered with blood; she crumpled and fell and died, as she had known she would after she first saw the enraged look on his face.

commentary on how blacks contribute to racial oppression

CHAPTER 2

A woman who had witnessed the murder from her kitchen window across the air well had gone down into the street, found a telephone and called the police precinct. The radio dispatcher had ordered the patrol car nearest to the scene of the crime to investigate.

The black Harlem detectives, Coffin Ed Johnson and Grave Digger Jones had been cruising south on Eighth Avenue from 125th Street, looking for known pushers, and they were approaching the intersection of 113th Street when the alarm was broadcast. They hadn't seen any known pushers, just the streets filled with addicts. It had made them sad. Addiction wasn't a crime, only possession was. And they knew none of the addicts had any of the shit left on them. The pushers kept well out of sight. So they were glad to break it off and investigate a killing for a change. At least the victim was already dead; not just dying on their feet like these mother-raping addicts, whom they could neither punish nor save. So they climbed to the fourth floor flat of T-bone Smith and found him lying on the dirty pallet in the bedroom, strung out on horse.

The door had been unlocked and after one glance at the body of the woman, which they had expected to find, they had stepped into the dirty, half-lit bedroom and found T-bone stretched out on the bed. He was still clad only in greasy black pants, with his torso bare to the waist. One look at his obsidian eyes, extended to the size of California prunes, and at the needle marks on his bare arms told them he was a main-liner of long standing, and that he had just indulged himself in a massive shot.

Coffin Ed reached down and tried to grip T-bone by the hair, but his hair was too short, so he grabbed him by the wrist and snatched him to his feet.

When Coffin Ed's face came into focus, T-bone muttered, "I were gonna call y'all, boss."

The tic began in Coffin Ed's face. He pushed T-bone toward a broken-legged kitchen table and grated, "Sit down."

Without speaking, Grave Digger went over and turned off the television.

T-bone looked at the chair and drew back in terror. "That chair got blood on it."

"It ain't yours," Coffin Ed said.

"But I'm gonna add some of his to it if he don't straighten up," Grave Digger threatened.

Coffin Ed pushed T-bone down into the bloody chair. His face turned gray with terror. He was too high to be terrified of the consequences of his crime, he was merely terrified of the blood.

"Why'd you kill her?" Coffin Ed asked.

"She were tryna shoot me," T-bone whined. Even in his terror, a sly look of cunning flitted over his face. He thought he knew what to tell the police.

Both detectives turned to look at the mutilated body for the first time. At the sight of the slashed and bloody carcass of what had, a short time before, been some kind of a black woman, their blood boiled with anger and revulsion. The sight of this violent death, following on the heels of a frustrating morning watching junkies, filled both of them with rage. Grave Digger's neck swelled until his collar choked him; Coffin Ed's burned face began to twitch. What kind of life had this black woman lived to deserve this bloody death, they wondered.

Finally they saw the gun spattered with gouts of congealing blood. Coffin Ed stuck the long, nickel-plated barrel of his .38 revolver through the trigger guard and used both hands to lift it onto the table. "U. S. Army," he observed. "But it ain't stamped," he added, after examining it for a moment.

Grave Digger also examined it with his gaze, but neither of them touched it with the naked hand. "With this gun?" he asked.

"Yassuh, boss, she aim it at me an' threaten to waste me 'n I cut her trying to 'fend myself."

"You been in the army?"

"Yassuh."

"And you thought this gun was loaded?" Coffin Ed asked.

"Where'd she get this gun?" Grave Digger asked.

"It weren't hers, someone sen' it to me."

"To you?"

"Yassuh, boss."

"Who?"

"I dunno, boss. A boy in uniform come here 'n knock on de do' an' say they flowers for me. But I knew they weren't no flowers 'cause they was too heavy."

"Where's the box it came in?"

"Over there, boss, but I knew soon's I felt it, it weren't no flowers."

In stepping over to retrieve the box from the far side of the room where the woman had knocked it trying to escape, Grave Digger noticed the printed instruction sheet lying on the floor, weighted down with blood. He picked it up and read it, and then passed it to Coffin Ed. After having read the printed message, they gave the box a cursory examination.

"Can you read?" Grave Digger asked T-bone.

Sight of the printed page once again filled T-bone with inexplicable terror. He seemed to be more frightened by the printed word than by the angry detectives and their guns. "Nawsuh, boss, but she read it to me."

"I'm going to read it to you again," Grave Digger said and read aloud the printed words: "*WARNING!!! DO NOT INFORM POLICE!!! LEARN YOUR WEAPON AND WAIT FOR INSTRUCTIONS!!! REPEAT!!! LEARN YOUR WEAPON AND WAIT FOR INSTRUCTIONS!!!*

WARNING!!! DO NOT INFORM POLICE!!! FREEDOM IS NEAR!!! You understand that?"

Coffin Ed looked across at Grave Digger. "Don't push him, Digger," he cautioned. "He ain't very bright."

"He's bright enough to know what I'm asking him," Grave Digger grated, and again he asked T-bone, "Did you understand what I asked you?"

"Yassuh, boss, you mean do I unnerstand what it say?"

"That's right, what did it say?"

"Well, it talk about stuff I don' go long wid, boss. She say the uprising, 'n that sort of shit. But I'se a law-abiding man an' I was gonna call the police."

"You were going to call the police and tell them about receiving the gun?"

"Yassuh, boss, leas' I were gonna go get 'em, 'n tell 'em." He was relieved to get himself in the right.

"And she tried to stop you?" Grave Digger persisted.

Coffin Ed was watching Grave Digger with disturbed emotions; he didn't know what Digger was trying to get at and he felt confused and uneasy. T-bone had grown uneasy too; at first he thought he had gotten himself in the right, but suddenly he was no longer sure.

"I di'n unnerstand you, boss."

"I asked you if she tried to stop you from going after the police."

"Yassuh, boss. Dass wut I sayin', she swore she waste me if I goes."

"And she aimed the gun at you?"

"Yassuh, boss."

"But you had been in the army and handled this type of gun and you knew it wasn't loaded."

"Nawsuh, boss," he denied vehemently. "I di'n know it weren't loaded."

"How'd you find out?"

"She pulled the trigger."

"And when you found out it wasn't loaded you pulled out your knife and cut her to death."

"Nawsuh, boss, I were jes' try'na get away to tell the police and she wanna stop me. She call me whitey's slave."

"What do you do for a living?" Grave Digger asked.

"I been looking for a job."

"What did she do?"

"She went out 'n did some housework downtown sommers."

"You mean she hustled around the lagoon in Central Park."

"Sometimes, maybe."

The whole of Grave Digger's head had begun to swell and his voice became tight and cotton-dry with rage. The veins in his temples roped as though air had been pumped into them.

"You lived off what this black woman made selling her body to white tramps," Grave Digger choked. "You lived off her faith and her sweat and her depravity."

Coffin Ed was watching him in alarm. He had never seen his partner lose himself in such a rage.

"Easy, Digger," he cautioned again. "Easy man. This black mother-raper ain't worth it."

But Grave Digger's head was roaring with fury and he didn't hear his partner. "And you wasted her because she wanted to be free."

T-bone began jerking with terror as though in death convulsions himself. "I were gonna tell is all," he whined through lips bone dry. "It were more for her than it were for me."

"You can tell her again, mother raper," Grave Digger rasped, his throat as dry as T-bone's lips.

"Digger!" Coffin Ed cried as Grave Digger drew back his pistol.

T-bone came up out of his seat like a terrified rat and met the descending butt of the long, nickel-plated pistol with an inadvertent sense of destiny. His body fell straight into the congealing blood of the woman he'd killed. Simultaneously, Grave Digger let out a long strangled sigh, almost as though he'd had a furious orgasm.

Coffin Ed was the first to break the frozen silence. "He weren't worth it, Digger."

Grave Digger looked down without regret at the body of the man he'd just killed and said, "He ain't now."

"But you shouldn't have done it, man. The commissioner is going to be on our asses."

"You ain't involved, Ed. I'll take my own medicine."

"Ain't involved? I'm here, ain't I? I'm your partner, ain't I? We're a team, ain't we? I'd killed him, too, man. I'd have just done it different is all."

"No, partner, I'm not going to let you stick your neck out for me. This was my own private feeling, my own private action. I don't ask you to feel like me, man, and I'm not going to let you share in the blame. I did it. I killed this black mother myself, I busted his skull alone, and I'd do it again. I did it because that woman looked something like my ma looked as I remember her, a poor black woman wanting freedom. And I'd kill any black mother on earth that was low enough to waste her for that. But I'm not going to let you share this feeling, man, because this is for my mama."

"Okay, Digger, it's yours and I ain't gonna try to share it, but you can't stop me from saying he drew his chiv on you, because that's what I'm going to say."

On sudden impulse Grave Digger put the bloodied instruction sheet in his pocket. "All I want you to do is just don't say nothing about this, Ed," he said. "Let's just keep it to ourselves until we find out more about where it is."

"Where what is?"

"Freedom."

"All right, partner, I'll be deaf, dumb, and blind. But it ain't going to be easy."

"Sure ain't."

the beginning of the fragmentation of the team

PLAN B

20

CHAPTER 3

Like many great institutions, CHITTERLINGS, INC. had come about by accident. At the beginning of the nineteenth century, the large area of swamp land bordering on Mobile Bay that was later reclaimed for the factory of CHITTER-LINGS, INC., was the property of an incompetent English slave owner, named Albert Harrison. Because a large section of the swamp was overgrown with canebrakes, he believed this land would be ideal for the culture of sugar cane that could later be sold to rum distilleries. So Harrison purchased five thousand acres for a pittance from a friend who knew a sucker when he saw one, and with the remainder of his inheritance purchased one hundred infirm, bargain-priced slaves, and built a large white, dreadfully uncomfortable mansion on the banks of the Tombigbee River.

Knowing little about the habits of slaves and even less about the responsibilities of ownership, he put his slaves to work clearing the canebrakes and expected them to feed and house themselves off the land. Before long, though, many of his slaves had joined the tribes of native Indians who gave the river its name and Harrison was left alone in the big uncomfortable house with his young wife and one old, decrepit slave who served as cook, valet, and housekeeper.

Sick with frustration and too ashamed of his ineptitude to face his neighbors, Harrison kept to his gloomy house, brooding all day and copulating with his young wife all night. In ten years they had eleven offspring, seven of them afflicted with congenital idiocy. His final hope of ever recouping his fortune disappeared with the death of his father in England and the subsequent loss of his credit. Finally, even his old Uncle Tom slave retainer vanished into the night. To put the capstone on his misfortunes, he discovered that his wife was dying from cancer of the womb.

One morning he awakened to a cacophony of his idiot children crying in hunger and his wife screaming in pain. He took down his old double-barreled shotgun, loaded it, and began systematically shooting them two at a time. He shot his wife first, not out of any altruism he may have possessed, but simply because she was nearest. The idiot children sat looking at him with open mouths and dull eyes, seeming to wait their turns, but the three girls and one boy who were mentally normal took to their heels in their ragged nightshirts, their little white asses shining in the morning sun. He took a couple of potshots at them as they fled toward the canebrake and winged the youngest, a skinny, freckled, tow-headed little girl of three, before the others got away. She had been shot in the calf of her left leg and couldn't move, so he left her lying in the sun, screaming in agony, while he dispatched the rest of the idiots. Then he walked out into the yard in his nightshirt and blew out her brains. Then came his final achievement in life. He reloaded the gun, sat on the back stairs with it held between his knees and, with its stock resting on the bottom step, pulled both triggers with his big toe, blowing off his face.

The orphaned children were taken in by a sympathetic neighboring family named Macpaisley, who were not much better off then the Harrisons had been, but who had at least been able to hang on to a few imbecile slaves. The eldest of the orphaned Harrisons was a girl nine and a half years old called Hope. The next born was a boy called "Lovely." Whether it was his real name or a nickname, no one ever knew, for his parents had been the sole authority on the subject. The other remaining child, the fifth born, was a five and a half year old girl named "Cotton Tail." If it was a nickname, it was at least appropriate, because if she hadn't run like a cottontail rabbit, she'd now be dead. All three of them were thin, towheaded children, with peaked, freckled faces and wild, frightened, blue-gray eyes.

The Macpaisleys had nine children of their own, three of them almost grown: Liam, a seventeen year old boy known as "Lim," Nora, a sixteen year old girl called "Nookie," and Little, a fifteen year old boy called "Li'l." The others were stairstepped down to a nameless infant.

Only the three eldest Macpaisley children showed any interest in the Harrison orphans. Lim, the eldest, kept sniffing around Hope trying to get a chance to "rut" her like his father did his mother. And Nookie kept taking out Lovely's little thing whenever they were alone and playing with it in the hope of getting it hard enough to stick into her "nookie," from which she got her name. Li'l, who was the nearest to an idiot of them all, just wanted to copulate with five-year-old Cotton Tail as he had seen the black slave, Jeb, do to a neighbor's sheep one day.

Mr. Macpaisley, a huge, red-bearded, bald-pated, pot-bellied dirt farmer of indisputable vigor but little ambition, after unsuccessfully attempting to grow sugar cane as affluent slave owners were doing, had settled on raising yellow yams, razorback hogs, and illiterate, unlovely, and unhealthy children with his wife, known locally as "Fertile Myrtle."

He had been fortunate to discover, while still solvent, that sugar cane wouldn't grow in the infertile swampland, but that razorback hogs thrived in the canebrakes on a diet of snakes and bamboo roots. Yellow yams grew wild on the bone-dry patches of arrid land. The combination of yams and stringy pork had not only proved salable, but profitable, besides supplying his family with almost their complete diet. His eleven infirm slaves had little to do other than dig up the yams and spear the razorbacks with sharpened sticks, and support his prestige as a slaveowner, which was actually their primary task.

Myrtle Macpaisley, a fading, gray-haired woman with lean, sagging breasts and a flabby, spreading figure, still retained her craving for a good "screw." She was famous for her proud and uninhibited boast that her husband "could rut like a nigger." To be sure, however, it is doubtful that Mrs. Macpaisley had ever had the opportunity to discover how a nigger rutted.

The three Harrison orphans grew up in the Macpaisley household where it was accepted that Lovely would inherit his father's swampland property upon reaching the legal age of maturity. Little happened to them during those years except that Hope bore Lim's child, but did not marry him. Lovely was repeatedly raped by Nookie but no offspring resulted, and little Cotton Tail acceded to Li'l's abnormal craving so often she had developed a preference for it to all other forms of copulation.

Yet fate had played a more diabolic joke on Cotton Tail than her volitional conversion to sodomy. She had become the most beautiful girl in the area, perhaps in all the South. At fifteen she was a blonde, blue-eyed dream with a body to stir a dead man. She was the most desirable girl along the entire coast of the Gulf of Mexico, surpassing even the Creole beauties. Handsome young suitors came from as far away as New Orleans to seek her hand in matrimony, many of whom were the heirs of fabulously wealthy estates with more than a thousand slaves.

The elder Macpaisleys were in a constant flutter, trying to arrange the most advantageous marriage for her to the wealthiest and most desirable of these young dandies. They had visions of accompanying her into the world of wealth and prestige, and these pretensions set their impoverished neighbors to comment that, "They think their shit don't stink no more."

But Cotton Tail was so cold to the advances of these young swains she soon acquired the reputation of being frigid. They lusted for her like dogs in heat, yet none had the imagination to discern in the spasmodic quivering of her buttocks the invitation so obviously posed. They called her a "teaser," and swore she masturbated, or copulated with her sisters or the Macpaisley girls. She was angered and frustrated because none had the gumption to take the pleasure she went to such pains to offer. Rebuffed by her scorn and anger, they gradually quit coming, and it was left to Li'l to satisfy the craving he had instilled in her.

The Civil War was in its last year when Lovely came of age and the elder Macpaisleys, finally conceding the failure of their plans for getting Cotton Tail married into wealth, unhesitatingly persuaded the three Harrison orphans to return to their homestead. Their sole possession was the shotgun neighbors had retrieved from their father's massacre. They hadn't returned to the house in seven years. It was like making an expedition to the unknown. Nevertheless, having abandoning all hope of getting Lim, to marry her, Hope took her six-year-old daughter, Aslip, with them. This was probably the most sensible course, since Lim was already the father of seven other tots in the area, two of whom were half-breeds, and he couldn't be expected to marry all the mothers.

By then the big, gloomy mansion their father had built on the banks of the Tombigbee was overgrown with foliage and was rotting into dust. The roof was falling in, the house had listed to one side, floorboards had caved in, and nests of cottonmouth water moccasins and sluggish rattlesnakes had made it their home.

The wooden pier Harrison had built into the bay for the transportation of his sugercane in the days of his hope had rotted and fallen apart. The floorboards had fallen into the water and been washed away. Only the decaying, water-logged timbers of the wooden pier that had been sunk into the river bed remained. The five thousand acres of cane-brake and swampland had become impenetrable.

The bloodstains of their murdered mother and little sisters and brothers were still visible on the rotting kitchen floor, the rusted stove, the glass and china and the pots and pans. The sheets, bedcovers, and mattresses, and even parts of the wooden floor had been eaten away by carnivorous insects. The massacred bodies had been removed, whether by kind neighbors or wild animals the orphans never learned. No skeletons remained.

Lovely shot into the nests of snakes, making great gaping holes in the floors and walls, but many snakes were killed and wounded. He battered the heads of the wounded with the gun butt and his sisters removed the bodies and piled them atop a stack of dry bamboo in the front yard and burned them.

They had no light or food and the water in the neglected

well was doubtless contaminated. For the first week they worked by day on the old house with borrowed tools to make it habitable and returned to the Macpaisleys' every night.

First they burned sulphur candles in all the rooms and closed and sealed the doors and windows the best they could in order to contain the sulphur fumes. Through this method, they killed all the animal life within the house. The next day they found the floor covered with the bodies of dead snakes, many of which were pregnant, dead rats, bats, flies, ants, moths, and a few birds. They built a giant bonfire to burn the carcasses and for many days following the entire area smelled as though a door to hell had opened.

With a hand saw, hammer, and nails, Lovely patched up the floors and boarded up all unneeded windows. All the rotted bedding and garments were burned, producing such an ungodly odor that it seemed that another door to hell had sprung ajar. Afterward they covered their beds with bamboo leaves. Within a week's time they had made two rooms liveable, but were still without light or water. None of them dared lay down on a bed without Lovely first prodding it thoroughly with a cocked and loaded gun. Snakes still found their way inside occasionally, because snakes seemed to like human companionship.

Finally they learned to safeguard themselves while sleeping by placing shards of mirrors strategically about the floor to trap insects on their surfaces and prepare a feast for any snakes that might invade during the night. They put quicklime into the well to purify the water and Lovely soon became adept at shooting the wild razorbacks and boars that wandered into the clearing. The Macpaisleys gave them a bushel of yams from time to time, and the sisters learned to gather the fresh bamboo shoots early in the morning and boil them with the fresh meat.

Thus, with the occasional help and companionship of the Macpaisleys, they managed to survive. They suffered most from the frustration of their sexual appetites. Finally Lovely hit upon the solution of sleeping with his elder sister, Hope. However, poor little Cotton Tail was left to languish in her depraved misery. It seemed perfectly logical for her brother to copulate with her sister, but she could hardly expect him to satisfy her abnormal lust, too. She suffered so in her caldron of unrequited passion that she was prepared to seduce a black slave, but there were no black slaves about who could be seduced.

Most of the slaves had heard about the Emancipation Proclamation via the grapevine, and many of them had taken to the bush. Those who remained were kept under lock and key by their irate masters. But the canebrakes of the Harrison plantation were too forbidding for the hardiest runaway slave, so Cotton Tail was denied her sexual satisfaction.

CHAPTER 4

The Harrison orphans had already lit the lantern and were just about to sit down to a supper of boiled pork, bamboo shoots, and yellow yams when a band of marauding Union soldiers appeared one day. The nine ragged, unshaven, red-eyed, savage-looking infantry soldiers came with loaded rifles into the kitchen from the dusk. The Civil War had been over for three months, but the Harrisons hadn't heard about it.

A glance was enough to tell them that the soldiers were the enemies of the South, and that they were bent on rape and plunder. With lightning-quick reflexes, Hope slapped her daughter, Aslip, from the table and hissed at the terrified child, "Run hide." The soldiers scarcely had time to realize the child's existence, so quickly did she vanish.

They weren't interested in her anyway. They wanted more mature women to rape and caches of gold and precious jewels to plunder. They had heard all about the fabulous riches of the slave owners and the wild beauty and hot passions of their women, but they had also heard that the slaves would be hidden in the woods, the treasures buried, the plantations neglected, the houses unpainted so as to appear dilapidated, and the women dressed in rags to hide their appeal.

At the Harrison plantation they found no more than they had expected; an overgrown plantation made to look neglected, the bearded young heir who had no doubt fought in the Confederate Army and was now disguised in civilian rags, and the women, maybe his wife and sister, one of whom was extraordinarily beautiful and desirable, both clad in the foulest and most repulsive rags. No one but an actress on the stage wore clothes as ragged as those. They weren't fooled. Doubtless the gold and jewels were buried nearby in the back yard. Since darkness was falling they'd just have time to take their pleasure with the women and force the man to reveal where his treasure was hidden before getting back to their company in Mobile in time to beat the midnight curfew.

They quickly bound Lovely to his kitchen chair and set about raping the two women, one in each room. Despite her unkempt hair and dirty face, Hope was found to be more than acceptable. Her body was white and sturdy, had good movements, gripped strongly, and joyously milked a man until he was thoroughly drained.

Cotton Tail, however, was something else again. When the first soldier approached her, she turned over on her beautiful young breasts and smooth milk-white belly and presented her dimpled buttocks. For a moment, the soldier thought he was back in the barracks, but he had never seen anything so delectable there. He had hoped to rape a virgin, but he took his pleasure where it was willingly offered and enjoyed it more than he thought possible.

From his chair in the kitchen, Lovely could see both of his sisters being raped. He didn't resent the rape of Hope so much, for he knew she welcomed a change. However, he was outraged when he saw his little sister, Cotton Tail, bestially prodded in the rectum as though she were a sheep. So great was his rage that he broke his bonds and leaped across the intervening space onto the back of the rutting soldier, but his mates snatched up their rifles and blew off the top of his head. Blood and brains splattered over the back of the offending soldier and droplets of the sticky goo dripped on Cotton Tail's bare skin.

Although Cotton Tail hadn't seen her brother attack her seducer, the sound of shooting shocked her. She was so terrified when she saw her murdered brother's body rolling across the floor that her limbs tightened convulsively and she experienced such an overwhelming ecstasy that she cried out in a loud, wailing moan.

The soldiers dragged Lovely's body out through the kitchen and threw it into the back yard. After cleaning up the more distracting gouts of blood and brains, they continued with their pleasure. Each soldier ravished both women and greatly enjoyed the contrast.

The women thought nothing of being raped nine times. They were as strong and willing at the end as they had been in the beginning. Their only regret was for the death of their brother, although they couldn't really think about it while being so energetically raped.

After the long session of rape, the soldiers were sated with pleasure. With the cessation of activity, the women began to grieve. The soldiers were straightening up their uniforms and buttoning their flies, preparatory to searching for the hiding place of any treasure when suddenly Aslip, Hope's little girl, burst into the room crying, "I been snake-bit, Ma."

She looked so appealing with her blue eyes glistening with tears and her face flushed from having run down the back stairs from her hiding place that the soldiers felt a revival of lust. She was certain to be a virgin, they thought, and two of them threw her to the floor. The sisters, outraged by this atrocity, turned on the soldiers and fought them like tigresses. They clawed the soldier's faces, tore at their eyes, and kicked them in the shins, but the soldiers finally overwhelmed them with superior numbers. They were restrained, three men to each woman, while the other three ravished the child in turn, her screams and convulsions exciting them all the more. It was not until a fourth soldier prepared to mount her that they realized she was dying. The soldiers fled into the night, their buttons still undone.

Maddened with grief and rage, Hope flew after them. Cotton Tail was left alone to administer to the dying child. She discovered the bite on the back of the child's left calf and tried desperately to suck out the poison, but it was too late. Aslip was already dead. Cotton Tail found her brother's shotgun and took the lantern upstairs to find the snake, but like the soldiers, it, too, had disappeared.

She thought of her sister then, and armed with the lantern and the gun, she went into the clearing and called Hope's name, but to no avail. She then followed the path that led to the Mobile road, but could find no sign of her sister or the maurading Union soldiers. She returned to the house and arranged Aslip's body neatly on her mother's bed, then dragged in the body of her brother and arranged it alongside the child. Then she fanned up the fire and made some "coffee" from dried wild berries that they were accustomed to drinking and sat up all night waiting for the return of her sister.

By dawn Hope still hadn't returned. Cotton Tail at first thought that Hope might have followed her ravishers into Mobile, but that didn't seem likely, considering her state of mind. It was more plausible that she had forced them to kill her. When the sun came up, Cotton Tail walked to the Macpaisley's farm and recounted the night's atrocities.

Macpaisley tried to get his son, Lim, to come with them to investigate, but Lim refused outright. He didn't want to be killed by the soldiers, too, he said.

Eight of Macpaisley's slaves, taking advantage of the confusion, had fled. Only three, feeble old male slaves, dreading the unknown world, had remained. With these three slaves and Cotton Tail, Macpaisley set out to look for Hope. First they returned to the house to see if she had returned in

Cotton Tail's absence, but the house, except for the dead, was deserted. Then the little party set out in the direction of Mobile, searching the woods and gullies flanking the road for her body or some sign of her existence. By the time they had reached Mobile, they had still found nothing. However, they learned there that the detachment of Union soldiers had left at dawn and there had been no woman matching Hope's description among the camp followers.

Returning to the house, Macpaisley put his slaves to work digging graves for Lovely and Aslip, after which he said a prayer over each before they were covered. The slaves made crude crosses of cane to mark their graves. It was while they were thus engaged that they found the first trace of Hope. In gathering dried cane at the fringe of the clearing, one of the slaves noticed a cotton rag clinging to a bamboo stalk that couldn't have been there for any length of time.

Macpaisley got down on hands and knees and studied the ground around the cane stalks. He found there bare footprints entering the canebrake, definitely establishing that Hope had returned from chasing the soldiers. But why had she gone into the canebrake? What could she have been doing? He walked slowly around the clearing, studying the ground inch by inch, but there were no other footprints, suggesting that she had been alone. The conclusion that she was still in the canebrake was a frightening one. No human being could remain alive in the canebrake with its legion of poisonous snakes, dangerous boars, poisonous insects, and the bears and cougars that were rumored to be in there.

PLAN B

"Maybe she was searching for the snake that bit Aslip," Cotton Tail suggested.

Macpaisley felt the hair rise on the nape of his neck. Definitely, she had gone crazy, he said to himself. All the signs pointed to it, and she had had plenty of reason for it. However, she was a white woman and had to be given a good Christian burial, so he ordered his slaves to go into the canebrake and find her body. The slaves looked at one another in terror and consternation. Their eyes rolled whitely and the black seemed to seep from their skin, leaving it gray-looking. They knew no one could ever have gone into that canebrake and come out alive. Macpaisley saw their hesitancy and aimed his shotgun at them. He threatened to shoot them if they didn't obey.

One of the slaves, braver than his companions, muttered defiantly, "Usses doan have to, us is free."

Macpaisley shot him instantly. The two others broke away, but they were old and neither of them was spry and agile enough to escape from any sort of fair shot. Macpaisley brought down one with a well-aimed shot to the base of the spine, but the other got out of sight while he was reloading. He could have run and caught up with him and killed him, too, but since he was a Catholic he decided to let him go.

Angered by the whole situation, he spent his fury and frustration on Cotton Tail. "Goddamned snotnose whore. Heah ah is lost all my slaves trying to do you cussed people a Christian service when you probably brought all you got down on yo'selves. Tryna fight off them wild randy soldiers 'bout a li'l pussy. Why didn' you gib 'em a li'l pussy, gib 'em all the pussy they wanted? Were it gonna hurt yuh? Now all but you is dead 'bout some pussy that ev'body got for nuthin—"

"It weren't that," Cotton Tail interrupted. "You think we'd get ourselves killed for that? It were 'cause they raped Aslip after she were snakebit and she died while they was raping her."

"Well hell Godalmighty, why didn't Hope have her out of the way?"

"She were, she come in after she were snakebit."

"They how'd Lovely git his ass killed?"

"I dunno, I weren't lookin'."

"Well, ah ain't gonna let you get my ass killed whilst you ain't lookin'. You jus' take yo' ass somewheres elst."

So Cotton Tail took her ass to New Orleans where she approached the madam of a whorehouse on Rampart Street.

"I wanna job as a whore," Cotton Tail said.

"Where's your man?" the madam asked her.

"I ain't got no man."

"What's your experience, then?"

"You mean as a whore? I ain't got no experience of charging for it."

"Amateur, eh?" the madam sneered. "We don't use no amateurs here, else all women would be whores."

"I can learn to charge," Cottontail said.

The madam looked at her appraisingly. "You got a speciality?" she asked.

"Oh yes, I got a specialty," Cottontail said.

And she had a specialty, indeed. She became famous throughout all New Orleans and on the ships at sea for her specialty.

"Bess piece of ass I had since my li'l mulatto nigger boy growed up," one discriminating former slave owner said, expressing the opinion of many other former slave owners with similar tastes, to say nothing of the opinions of others who had never been slave owners.

But after she had been in the whorehouse less than ten years, she was bought by a rich Arab who had made his fortune in the black slave trade. He took her back to his native land and installed her in his harem particularly because of her specialty.

Thus the Harrisons disappeared from the face of America, but the Harrison estate with its five thousand acres of totally useless canebrakes, swamp land, and its rotting, foetid, snake-ridden mansion remained. The place was always known to the end of its existence as the "Harrison Place." In the vicinity it gained a reputation for being haunted, and no native in his right mind could be forced within sight of it, even at the point of a gun.

However, a few itinerant tramps, white casualties of the Civil War, and freed slaves with nowhere else to sleep, put up there for short intervals, living off the razorback hogs, steaks from fat snakes, and bamboo shoots. Of course, none of these knew of its reputation as a haunted house.

It remained untenanted and unvisited by ordinary human beings until 1917, when it was surveyed by a crew of engineers to see if it could be converted into a naval drydock. By then, a railroad line connecting Mobile to Montgomery had been built along its western boundary, and a short distance further west a highway had been built to Meridian, Mississippi.

However, the engineers turned it down and, after World War I, it was put up for auction for unpaid back taxes. But no one could be found who wanted it, even for free, so it remained uninhabited until Tomsson Black got out of prison and bought it for the home factory of Chitterlings, Inc., because he had heard stories about the razorback hogs with piquant chitterlings.

Tom's son, Black

CHAPTER 5

Abrupt shift

The next to arrive were crews from the police cruisers which had been dispatched from the precinct. But the detectives outranked all the uniformed car cops and everyone stood around waiting for someone with more authority. If the white cops thought it strange that both the man and woman were dead, none of them said so.

The first man of authority to appear was a bored detective from homicide who fired his questions at the two black detectives because no one else was alive who might know anything.

"Where'd she get the gun?"

"He said it was sent to him."

"By whom?"

"He said he didn't know. A messenger brought it and disappeared. There is no address of the sender and no name or address of the florist on the box it came in."

The homicide detective, whose name was Rankin, picked up the florist's carton and examined it. It told him nothing. But inside, packed neatly in the excelsior, he found two hundred rounds of ammunition in four boxes that fitted snug to the bottom of one end.

"Here's the ammunition," he said unnecessarily.

No one disputed him.

He turned to the automatic rifle.

"Army gun," he stated. "Stolen from some camp no doubt." But on further examination, he added, "But the camp's stamp is missing." And still later he observed, "No marks of any kind. Not visible, anyway. Maybe the lab will find some inside. Mmmm, that's strange," he mused.

"Sure is," Coffin Ed agreed.

Grave Digger threw him a warning look, but Rankin ignored him, and turned to the corpse of the man. He bent down and examined him as best he could without touching him. Then he looked from one black detective to the other. "Which one of you men killed him?"

"We don't have to answer your questions," Coffin Ed flared. "We're detectives with the same rank as yours."

"You'll have to answer someone's," Rankin warned. "Because this man was killed after this woman was dead and he didn't hit himself on the head."

"That's as may be. But we'll report the circumstances surrounding his death to our superior officer in our precinct."

"And at the same time I'll report my observations to my superior officer at the homicide bureau in the DA's office."

Grave Digger hadn't said anything.

The M.E.'s assistant arrived, shedding dandruff from his long black hair over the shoulders of a blue flannel suit that had seen better days. He went to work examining the bodies, ignoring everyone, like a medical Hamlet absorbed in his private horror. Causes of death in both instances were obvious, but only one obvious murder weapon had been discovered; it was a springblade knife to which were sticking gouts of congealed purple blood. The blunt instrument responsible for the crushed skull of the male corpse was not discovered.

The Harlem precinct was inclined to handle the killing as just another homicide in Harlem. Lieutenant Anderson accepted the veracity of his two ace black detectives, whose report on the killing of the woman was substantiated by the report of the assistant Medical Examiner and the observations of the homicide detective, Rankin. But Rankin added to his report that the death of the male victim appeared to result from a blow inflicted by one of the arresting officers, and, as such, demanded an investigation at the precinct level.

Captain Brice joined Lieutenant Anderson the following day to listen to the statements of the two black detectives.

"What I want to know is just what happened to cause one of you men to club this man over the head," Captain Brice said with an open mind.

"Nothing happened," Grave Digger said tightly. "I just lost my head and hit the black mother with my pistol butt. I just hit him too hard is all."

"He attacked Digger with his knife," Coffin Ed amended. "He had shot himself full of horse after he had knifed the woman and when we got there he was in a murderous state of excitement. He snatched up the bloody knife and started into Digger who was in front, and Digger just banged him once lightly to cool him down. He just hit him too hard is all."

"Doesn't know his own strength," Anderson put in, smiling.

"Sounds to me like an open and shut case of self defense," Captain Brice admitted.

He appeared willing to drop the inquiry and accept the self-defense verdict. One more dead nigger meant very little to Captain Brice, and it saved the state the cost of convicting him for the murder of the woman. But Coffin Ed couldn't stop talking.

"Yeah, some of these brothers are dangerous as blind snakes when they get high. And that brother had been mainlining for years."

But Captain Brice didn't agree with his diagnosis. It wasn't that the captain disagreed with the fact that the brother had gone mad after having killed the woman and had charged an armed detective with the bloody knife. That was ample justification for killing him. He was willing to accept it, whether it was true or not. But he disagreed, on purely technical grounds, that such action could be attributed to a massive shot of heroin.

"Heroin is made from morphine," he lectured. "And morphine, like all opium derivatives, is a sedative. So heroin is a sedative and not a stimulant. And if this man took a

P L A N   B

43

massive shot of heroin after killing the woman, it was to quiet his nerves, not excite them. And whether he took it for that purpose or not, that is what it would have done. It might have put him to sleep, but it wouldn't have incited him to charge an armed detective with a bare knife."

Anderson didn't agree. He had come up in the school of the crazed drug addict exploding into fits of incredible violence.

"Johnson doesn't claim the heroin stimulated the man as much as it produced a state of dementia. The man who attacked Jones was demented more than incited."

"Heroin doesn't make an addict any more demented than excited," Captain Brice argued. "Unless, of course, it's been cut with an alkaloid with a toxic content, such as various brands of roach powder; and that could only happen by the addict cutting it himself. Which couldn't happen in Harlem because by the time horse gets up here it has been diluted so thin with sugar of milk you could use it on a breakfast cereal."

Well, sir, all that might be true," the lieutenant conceded. "But I don't understand what you're trying to get at."

"I'm just trying to say if Jones busted that nigger's skull," he went on stubbornly, "it wasn't because that nigger was charging him with a knife. As long as I've been on this Harlem beat I know that there's no nigger who's going to charge an armed cop with a bare knife because he's had a shot of horse."

"Well, for whatever reason," Anderson contended, trying to save the day.

But Captain Brice had grown inflexible about his expertise on black character.

"For any reason," he concluded flatly.

"What you're saying is that Jones just killed this man without sufficient justification," Anderson spelled it out.

Captain Brice looked Grave Digger in the eye. "Yes, that's what I'm saying."

"In that case, we have no choice but to discipline him."

"No choice," the captain agreed.

As a consequence, Grave Digger was suspended from the force until his case could be reviewed by the commissioner's disciplinary committee.

so it becomes a RACE thing & Ed said too much, MZD Whitey MZD

The automatic rifle was sent down to the laboratory at police headquarters. There were no fingerprints on the gun, shells, or packing except those of the corpses and the various police officers who had handled them. That in itself wasn't unusual; no one in their right senses was going to leave identifying evidence on a gun destined to figure in a crime. But there were no manufacturer's marks of any kind on the gun, inside or out, which was more alarming. But the most alarming discovery of all was the lack of manufacturer's marks on the shells. All cartridges carry the manufacturer's trade mark. And they were too well-finished to be home-made. Everything pointed to this gun being made for an assassin.

But what puzzled the political experts was why it was sent to this ignorant black man. It would have made sense if it had been sent to anyone who could have been considered as a potential assassin of the president, or some other well-known politician, who were the only people assassinated in the United States. They could have correlated the fact of it being sent to a potential assassin of a black politician, for in recent years they had moved into the target area, too. But this ignorant, black, Uncle Tom bastard couldn't be considered as a potential assassin on any account. And what was more, he would never have committed any crime of violence where an automatic gun of this type was needed. From what was known of him, he had been a chickenshit drug addict, a halfass pimp, a wholehearted Uncle Tom who would never have injured a white man for any reason, for he considered whitey as his meal ticket; and he was not only non-political, but he was actually afraid of politics, which is the case with many people who can't read or write.

In the end it was this train of thought that dispelled all their budding alarms: whichever way you looked at it, it wasn't anything but a nigger mess, and it had never been intended to be anything else. Whoever had sent this gun to T-bone Smith had other intentions than his assaulting a white man, for T-bone Smith was as incapable of assaulting a white man as he was capable of assaulting his black woman, and in the final analysis, that was all that mattered.

dismissal of complexities of race politics

CHAPTER 7

"specific" time

It was eleven-thirty one Saturday night in August, on Eighth Avenue in Harlem, ten days after the incident of the murdered black woman, and the unmarked gun which resembled an M-14 U. S. Army infantry automatic rifle.

No one can visualize what Eighth Avenue is like who hasn't seen it. First, none of the residents has gone away on vacation, either to the seashore or the mountains, as is the case with most other New Yorkers. In fact, none of the residents has ever dreamed of going away during his vacation even in the wildest flights of his imagination. A few daring souls might get out to Coney Island, but most of these will be of the younger generation. For the most part the residents just sit in their squalor and swelter. There is no relief. Outside is the same as inside, night time is the same as day time. All the energy is steamed from the sweating, stinking bodies, and the will to move or do something about it, if there were anything to be done, is evaporated from the brain. The only relief which comes plausibly and facilely is to stupefy both body and brain with drink and drugs.

For the squalid Harlem slums do not have the same kind of squalor as the squalor of the black ghettos in the warmer climes, such as those in Rio, Miami, Capetown, or even Watts. The squalor of the Harlem slums is more comparable to the squalor of the black ghettos of Chicago, Detroit, Cleveland, and Philadelphia. For the slum buildings of Harlem were not designed for blazing heat, but for bitter cold; in fact they were designed for the bitter cold and the matter of the heat was completely ignored. Perhaps as a consequence, the heat of Harlem's slums is far hotter than the slums of Rio. The brick and concrete buildings, the concrete pavements, the macadamized streets, unrelieved by tree or shrub, and even the black skin of the black people, absorbs the heat of the sun, the heat radiations from motor vehicles, the heat generated by strong alcoholic drinks, loud voices, and fatty foods, and stores it up in much the same manner as scientists are endeavoring to store up the heat of the summer sun for use in locations with cold and sunless winters—the difference being that this heat, which is stored in the squalid slum environs and dirty black bodies of the residents of Eighth Avenue, merely serves to sizzle them in the summer when they least need it and vanishes in winter when they suffer from the bitter cold of these same environs.

As a consequence, the residents of Eighth Avenue and its

environs come out into the street at night seeking relief in the dark which looks cooler because they can't see the heat radiations of the day. It is a well-known fact that in primitive cultures the dark has always been considered cooler than the light, night cooler than the day. And this is still true in many parts of the world where the sun is the chief source of all heat. In Southern California, Florida, the French, Spanish, and Italian Riveras, and similar resort areas, there is a tremendous difference in temperature between sunny days and black nights.

But there is no practical difference whatsoever between day and night on Eighth Avenue in Harlem. The difference was made by the residents thinking it. So the residents were out in the streets, hopping from one cheap bar to another, drinking bottled heat and getting hotter. Or they were sitting on the stoops of their slum tenements, or on broken chairs on the sidewalks propped against the hot, crumbling walls, making themselves hotter for the exertions of their loud voices. Or they were packed like sardines into their many horsepowered jalopies, roaring from block to block, polluting the air with the hot gasoline fumes from exhausts, and sweating in the streams of heat blowing up from the engines. Or if they were young enough, they were heating themselves from their violent games, played between the stinking garbage cans. The coolest of the residents were the junkies, which is where the expression "Keep cool, fool," came from. The horse in their bloodstreams had calmed their nerves and made them so aloof and "cool" they didn't notice the heat, or even the squalor. That is why so many of them were junkies.

Unfortunately, it was not only unbearably hot, but it stank. Whether the heat would have been more bearable had it been perfumed is one of those stupid questions like, "which is more destructive, fire or water?" The fact is, it wasn't perfumed. It stank from rotting food in both garbage cans and kitchen cabinets, from animal offal in the streets and human urine on the stairs and hallways, from half-burnt gasoline and half-burnt hair. It stank from body odor—B. O. to you—underarm sweat, unwashed vaginas, unclean beds, rotting semen, unflushed feces, from the mating odors not only of black people but from black bugs, gray rats, black cats; it stank from the habitation of the many bugs between the walls—bed bugs, cockroaches, ants, termites, maggots—if you don't think the habitations of bugs stink, you should go to the zoo. It stank from the yearly accumulations of thousands of unlisted odors embedded in the crumbling walls, the rotting linoleum, the decayed wall paper, the sweaty garments, the incredible perfumes, the rancid face creams and cooking fats, the toe jam, the bad breath from rotting or dirty teeth, the pustules of pus. It stank from gangrenous sores, maggoty wounds, untended gonorrhea, body tissue rotten from cancer or syphilis.

The residents thought the air was fresher and cleaner and more pure outside than inside. But this was not so. In fact, as the French would say, *au contraire*. Outside there were all the impurities generated by their worn-out automobiles, their brimming garbage cans, the dog shit and cat shit, the putrefying carcasses of rats and cats and dogs and sometimes of meat too rotten even for the residents to eat, which had been tossed into the gutter for the animals. But some of it was too stinking even for hungry animals. And there were also the additional impurities from all the neighborhood food and merchandize stores, from the bars and restaurants, from the barber shops and beauty parlors.

Nevertheless, the residents thought it was cooler outside and that the air was more pure. "Honey, I'm going outside 'n sit in the cool for a spell 'n git a bit of fresh air." Therefore, on this Saturday night in August, they were all outside on the street, enjoying the cool and inhaling the fresh air.

see the irony + the ignorance of their deluded state

That same Saturday, two big, red-faced, uniformed white cops were driving slowly down the middle of the street in a police cruiser to impress these people with the meaning of law and order. It wasn't so much they intended to bring about law and order as it was to frighten these people into respecting it. But since this noble purpose was presumed for them instead of by them, in reality they were thinking less of law and order than the highly amusing sights from the police car. And because this assignment was not only boring but repulsive, they sought diversion in the really funny spectacle of terrified black junkies trying to make themselves invisible, as though they weren't already invisible to the great law-abiding mass of the nation's citizens.

They were new on this particular roving patrol covering the more squalid slum streets of the ghetto, which had formerly been attended by Grave Digger Jones and Coffin Ed Johnson. But Coffin Ed was incapacitated and Grave Digger had been suspended. The day following Grave Digger's suspension, Coffin Ed had fallen into an uncovered manhole while off duty and had injured his knee so severely he could barely stand, much less undergo the rigors of patrolling the kinkier slum streets of Harlem in the late hours of the night. Moreover, since an uncovered manhole might be legally construed as negligence on the part of the city, the officials thought it was best to let sleeping dogs lie, or rather injured dogs limp.

Lieutenant Anderson genuinely sympathized with him for more reasons than his injured knee, and let him take over the telephone complains of the black citizenry, a job that wasn't very difficult since black citizens had so few telephones. The white detectives in the squad room avoided him as though he had come down with a contagious disease instead of an injured knee, and, sad to say, there was no longer as much good American fun in the squad room as there had been in his absence. Which was a pity, for circumstances were proving that the black citizens of Harlem were as funny as ever.

In fact, the two blonde cops in the cruiser, Pan and Van, were laughing to beat all hell as they coasted down Eighth Avenue in the heat of the night.

I'm going to write a book," said Van, "and call it *Niggers is niggers is niggers*."

"Those black junkies remind me of hermit crabs scuttling to sea," said Pan.

"If I could put those junkies on the stage in Capetown, I could make a fortune," said Van.

"You'd need to give out baseballs to throw at them," said Pan.

"The only thing is the audience couldn't stand the stink," said Van.

"Yeah, there's something to be said for the gas chambers," said Pan.

"The stink blew away," said Van.

"Give them a burst from the siren," said Pan.

Instead there was a burst from an automatic weapon from the front window of a third floor tenement and the windscreen of the police cruiser exploded in a burst of iridescent safety glass. Not to mention the fact that Pan and Van were riveted to their black plastic seats by a row of 7.62 calibre rifle bullets that passed through their diaphragms. If they found anything funny about this "happening," they never said. But still the cruiser kept cruising slowly down the street and still the rifle bullets rained on it, puncturing the roof, shattering the side windows, pounding the drooping blonde heads into splinters of bone and blobs of soft gray brain tissue.

Suddenly the naked torso of a black man holding an army rifle appeared in the window shouting jubilantly, "I done blowed them goldilocks back to whiteyland!"

"Sweet Jesus!" some black woman screamed, whether in terror or rejoicing no one knew.

The black brothers and sisters out for a breath of "fresh" air in the "cool" of the night fled as though from the blazing evil itself, and the bullet pocked police car with the red and gold corpses of the two bullet-riddled cops kept cruising slowly down the street, as though it were the devil pursuing them.

"Come back, brothers," the rifle-armed brother yelled. "They ain't no danger to you."

But the brothers didn't believe him; no more did the sisters. They ran frenziedly in all directions, hiding in corners, doorways, behind vehicles, underneath parked cars and other dark places they thought to be safe, which had been abandoned a moment before by other brothers who considered them unsafe. No truer words describing their flights of panic were ever said than Joe Louis's immortal observation about Billy Conn: "He may run but he can't hide." The black citizens on Eighth Avenue in the environs of the shooting were running to beat all hell, but they couldn't find any place to hide. A black brother had mowed down two white cops. No matter how commendable this extravagant action might be, the plain fact was it cast them all in danger. They felt for him, all right, they prayed for him, but they didn't want to bleed for him. They felt for him but they couldn't reach him. In fact, they couldn't get away from him fast enough, and that was the trouble.

Because other police cruisers were coming like the avengers, their sirens screaming like escaped souls from hell, their red eyes blinking like Martian space ships. At first it was the sight of them that was so terrifying. No police in the history of the world looks as dangerous and acts as violent as the

American police. Before a shot was fired, black brothers and sisters were shitting in their pants. All these black people, who had protested in one way or another against being considered invisible by the white citizenry, would have given anything to have been invisible then.

The white cops in the cruisers roared up beside their bullet-pocked mate which had crashed into a wall, and looked at the blood-spattered corpses of their colleagues with half their skulls blown off, then looked around for the nearest black brother to start making him pay.

But the half-naked brother in the third floor window with the automatic rifle began shooting at the cops as though they were scavenger birds, and knocked three of them down before the others had scrambled for cover. Crouched behind their cruisers, the cops began blazing away in unison with their .38 calibre police specials. But the big 7.62 calibre slugs from the rifle were chopping the police cruisers apart systematically. The cops couldn't get to their wounded colleagues who lay on the pavement bleeding. But they kept peppering away at the windowsill in the tenement, behind which the brother was kneeling, blazing away with his rifle which he had rested on the windowsill.

It was the black citizens who were producing most of the drama. In panic-stricken terror, while the lethal bullets were sailing overhead, they had crawled across the filthy pavements into the equally filthy doorways and hallways and stairways of the hot, airless, filthy tenements, where they lay packed on the dirty floors, smelling stale urine, trembling in the stink of their own terror. Moaning, groaning, praying, and muttering vile curses while the gun battle raged outside, and the graffiti scratched and drawn on the decaying, yellowing walls looked down upon them.

An anthropoligist might be more interested in the graffiti inside than in the gun battle outside, or even in the sweating bodies of the black people squirming on the floors. Why do slum dwellers express themselves in graffiti depicting exaggerated genitals, he might ask himself. Why always genitals? Why oversized genitals? Why are black slum dwellers obsessed with these enlarged genitals, penises as big, comparitavely, as telephone poles, and heads as small as cocoanuts? What are they trying to tell themselves? That as humans their heads might be small in the white man's sight but their unseen genitals were as big as field artillery? But within the sound of the gunfire outside, their genitals had actually shrunk to the size of match sticks and peanuts.

By now, there were more than thirty police cruisers parked at all angles about the street, their red beacons blinking, but not a cop was in sight. They were all crawling about the paved street in the lee of the automobiles, shooting around the wheels, the hoods, and the trunks. Several tried to find a way to get inside the tenement from the back, but the tenements had been built back to back with the tenements on Manhattan Avenue without any thought of service or ventilation, and to reach the black maniac on the third floor, the cops would have to enter downstairs from the street. And that would entail crossing the deserted strip of sidewalk between the police cruisers and the doorway, through a hail of 7.62 calibre slugs that were slowly ripping the cars apart in lieu of other targets. After which they would have to walk over the sweating, stinking bodies of the black citizens who were packing the floors of the hallway and stairway from wall to wall. None of the cops opted for this solution, and one could scarcely blame them, in view of the fact that their three colleagues, who had been shot down at first, were by now ripped into shreds.

Some climbed into the windows of the tenements across the street and some to the roofs, but the firepower of the black brother's automatic rifle was so brutal it knocked out the windows, frames, bricks from the wall, and huge stones from the cornices of the tenements where the cops were lurking, so not one was so foolhardy as to show enough of himself to draw a bead on a target. Obviously, they were all outgunned by this one automatic rifle in this black man's hands. They were infuriated and frustrated themselves, for a change. They sent for riot guns, but it did not take them long to discover that ordinary riot guns were ineffective in the face of the brutal weapon this black man had. This weapon had been designed to kill under all circumstances, and the cops were loathe to prove the point. They sent for tear gas guns, but none got a chance to use them. As soon as they were pushed into view, they were hit and destroyed and blown out of sight.

CHAPTER 9

Lieutenant Anderson and Captain Brice had been at the scene for quite a while, but they had stayed clear of the gunfire and out of sight. Every now and then, Captain Brice's megaphoned voice could be heard issuing instructions that were too dangerous to obey. Coffin Ed sat in the car with them because of his injured knee.

Once Captain Brice asked him, "What would you do, Johnson?"

"I'd give them better housing," Coffin Ed began. "Better schools, higher wages—"

"I mean about this nigger," Captain Brice snapped.

"If it was me, I'd quit thinking about him as a nigger and start thinking about him as sick," Coffin Ed replied.

"He's going to be sicker than that shortly," Captain Brice said. "He's going to be dead."

"I'm no good here," Coffin Ed said, and he climbed painfully out of the captain's car.

"Go back to the precinct," Lieutenant Anderson said kindly, "and answer the telephone."

Shortly Captain Brice was on the telephone to the Chief Inspector down at police headquarters, after which he instructed the cops staked out underneath their cruisers. "Don't try to get him anymore. I've got help coming. I don't want any more of you men to get injured. Just contain him, that's all, just don't let him get away. If you see any black man trying to get out of those buildings, shoot him on sight."

The cops heard this order and remembered it. They were literal minded, and they did not see any extenuating circumstances, any kind of mitigating behavior. That was for judges and juries. They were cops, and cops were responsible for law and order; cops were supposed to arrest criminals and offenders of this law and order, shoot them if they resisted or tried to escape. A cop is a cop, not a welfare worker, a city planner, a sociologist. If black people lived in slums, that wasn't the cop's fault; the cop's duty was to see that they obeyed the law and kept the order, no matter where they lived. It was coincidental that rich and educated white people who lived in large, roomy, airy houses, in clean, fresh, well-kept neighborhoods were more likely to keep the law and the order, but cops didn't have so much to do in these neighborhoods.

So when Captain Brice instructed the cops, "If you see any black man trying to get out of any of these buildings, shoot him on sight," he must have believed the cops would obey him or he wouldn't have given them the order. Unless of course, he was a fool, a windbag, a jokester, or simply ineffective, none of which precinct captains in New York are apt to be.

There was a lull in the shooting, during which the naked torso of the black man who had been shooting from the third floor window became vaguely highlighted by the street lamps as he peered cautiously up and down the deserted street, at the pocked and pitted police cruisers, at the darkened windows of the tenements across the street, at the skyline of the opposite roof. He held his rifle loosely pressed to his shoulder, ready to shoot at anything that moved. But nothing moved. Not even the polluted, cordite-stinking air, which had become unbearably hot from the explosions of gunfire. His black features were indiscernable against the background, but the whites of his eyes were shaped like the crescent of a new moon, just like white people say. One couldn't see the shine of his pearly teeth for the simple reason that he kept his mouth shut. But no doubt they were there, hidden behind his red lips and his blue gums. All that could be seen of him was the oily glint of his muscular torso, gleaming like a freshly-cast bronze in a pitch-dark room.

Several of the more venturesome brothers on the floor of the street-level hallway crawled to the doorway and looked out, but from their worm's-eye view, they could see the immobile cops lying beneath the bullet-riddled cruisers and the dark blue-steel gleam of the .38 police specials in their hands. Needless to say, they drew back hastily, like worms sighting birds.

So they didn't see the bug-shaped tank coming up the middle of Eighth Avenue from the direction of downtown, looking about with its one eye at the end of a 105 mm cannon, like some kind of strange insect from outer space. The police had boasted of having a sophisticated weapon which could quell any riot imaginable. If this was it, it didn't look sophisticated in the common usage of the word, but it certainly looked impregnable. No human life was visible within it. It was shaped like a turtle with an insect's antenna. It moved on rubber-treaded caterpillar tracks. It didn't make any noise. It came quickly and silently, as if it knew where it was going and was in a hurry to get there.

When the brother with the 7.62 calibre automatic rifle first noticed it, it was almost level with his window. He peppered it with a startled burst from his brutal gun, but the 7.62 calibre bullets richocheted off its smooth round shell of bullet-proof alloy without any effect. The brother ducked. And just in time. The 105 mm cannon fired with a sound like artillery in a war, and the shell passed above him and hit the back wall of the darkened room, and blew the wall out, the ceiling out, the wall beyond out, the ceiling beyond out, and laid waste the entire four-room apartment from front to back in a burst of flame as bright as a lightning bolt. The impact shook the flimsy building from top to bottom like the tremor of an earthquake. The half-naked brother was covered with falling plaster and white plaster dust. The flat lay in a shambles of blasted walls, ripped-out ceilings, exposed beams, rubbish-covered floors, as though the wreckers had been at it.

Down below, the noise sounded to the frightened black people lying packed side by side on the floor of the entrance hallway like the clap of doom. From them rose a litany of muffled screams, moans of dread, whines of terror, curses of despair. The plaster and plaster dust showered down over them, splotching them with white, as though they were turning white with terror. William Faulkner would have been vindicated in his description of black skin turning the gray of wood ashes.

En masse, they squirmed toward the back of the hallway, but they couldn't escape by the back door because there wasn't any back door. Nor did anyone attempt to go up because that was where the demolition was coming from. What they wished to do was sink beneath the floor, but even though the jerry-built tenement might crumble beneath the cannon blasts, still the floors were strong enough to keep the black people imprisoned.

Nothing had been seen or heard of the black brother with the gun since the first cannon blast, but the cannoneers deemed it expedient to keep on cannonading, in the scorched-earth tradition of the U. S. Army, until any and all possible opposition had been eliminated. They had no intention of unnecessarily risking the lives of red-blooded American cops to capture one lone black maniac, that's why they had the cannon. So they kept blasting through the front windows with the 105 mm explosive shells until the jerry-built tenement began to crumble and disintegrate, like those enemy strongholds in World War II films being decimated by the artillery of our side.

As the flimsy walls and floors began to crumble and fall, dislocated beams and hunks of wall and flooring began to shower down upon the terrified black people lying on their bellies in the stinking dark of the entrance hallway. The black people bolted in terror out onto the dangerous, deserted street. They came out screaming, mouths stretched open, nostrils flaring, eyes walled with white, black skin splotched with white like patches of war paint, pissing and shitting themselves from fear, fleeing for their lives.

Whether the white cops hiding beneath the scattered police cruisers thought they were painted black savages on the war path, or whether they just thought of Captain Brice's instructions ("If you see any black man trying to get out of any of those buildings, shoot him on sight") is a factor which was never determined. The fact is they suddenly rose up from their hiding places and began shooting the fleeing black people down. White cops could never tell black men from black women, as has been evidenced in the Sharpsville massacre in South Africa.

But as the dead piled up and the shouts and screams of pain and terror could be heard above the roar of the gunfire, it was then, as a subsequent inquiry established, that the white cops lost their cool and became animals, killing people for the sheer pleasure of killing; killing black people who died with the fatalism of animals.

PLAN B

Either the black brother with the automatic rifle sensed what was happening on the street below or else became crazed by the screams of his terrified brothers—and sisters—for suddenly he leapt to his feet and stood in the open window on what must have been the only section of the flooring left in the room which could hold his weight. Ignoring the rifle in his right hand, which he had discovered was useless against the tank, he beat his chest with his left fist like a male gorilla and shouted in a loud, defiant black voice:

"I'll fight you white motherfuckers; I'll fight you one by one, I'll fight you with anything you wanna fight with; I ain't scared of you white motherfuckers."

No sooner had the words left his lips (almost as though the cannoneers had waited politely for him to finish), than he was struck in the chest by a 105 mm shell, and his body exploded. Some of the pieces of bloody flesh and splintered bones and loose teeth were blown out through the front window in which he had been standing and rained down onto the black corpses piled below. And those were the only pieces ever recovered to establish the fact of his existence. And the rifle which he had held was so badly damaged it was found useless for providing clues of any kind.

The immediate horror was so great the mind could not accept it. The mind recoiled from it. Some of the white cops found themselves laughing uncontrollably. But law and order had been restored to the vicinity of Eighth Avenue.

CHAPTER 10

Tomsson Black first learned about the razorback hogs with piquant chitterlings from another black convict in for rape, too, who slept next to him on the same Alabama chain gang. Some years previous, this convict, whose name was Hoop, had hidden out for several weeks in the old Harrison place and lived on the only diet possible of pork, snake, and bamboo shoots. At that time, Hoop had killed a redneck in the area named Atmore Macpaisley, doubtless a descendant of the slave-owning Macpaisleys, who had tried to make him fuck a mule in order to prove that a nigger was the only animal who could breed with a mule.

Afterward he had hidden from the posse in the snake-infested canebrakes until it became safe enough for him to come out to the old, dilapidated, rotten, mildewed house. Hoop said he had figured out that the chitterlings tasted so "strong"—*strong* was his word for them—because razor-backs ate so many snakes and fish. He said he had seen them pick up water moccasins, bite them in two, and continue eating them unruffled with the head of the snake biting them until it was eaten up, too.

It had given him gooseflesh, he said, the greedy way those razorbacks devoured live snakes. But they ate live fish in the same way, he said, just like bears did. Only the razorbacks ate the entire fish, head and all, while bears just bit out the bellies. He swore he had seen these razorback hogs diving for fish in the fetid, shallow swamps the same way pelicans did. He had seen a lot of pelicans fishing in the Okefenokee Swamp of Florida, but the razorbacks on the Harrison place could outfish them two to one.

The razorbacks would duck their heads beneath the scummy water and never come up without a fish, or an eel, or a snake. Hoop said he had seen hogs eat snakes ever since he was a child, but that was the first time he had ever seen hogs eat live fish. "Course, if you come to think about it, if a hog would eat a snake, it'd eat a fish, or anything else," he said.

He said the reason he began cleaning and cooking the chitterlings and eating them instead of the meat of the hog was because he was scared of being poisoned by all the venom the snake bites had left in the meat.

Both Tomsson Black and Hoop were serving life for raping white women. But there, the similarity ended. For one thing, Hoop had two or three murder charges waiting for him when he got through serving life for rape.

For another thing, Hoop was an older man with a different background and a different outlook on life. Hoop was forty-five years old, with a sagging belly, powerful, sloping shoulders, and a wet-black, moon-shaped face lit by twinkling white crescents and topped by a shiny bald pate. He had the misleading appearance of childish jollity, but he was neither childish nor jolly. Born and raised in the backwoods of the Deep South, he was a violent, dangerous man, with the sneaky lethality of a cottonmouth moccasin who can bite you to death under water. He was the type of man you'd say had never been a child. He had been raping women and murdering men ever since he left the cradle, or what had passed for one in the sharecropper's shack where he was born. And he had killed more nigger-hating rednecks and peckerwoods in the south than pellagra.

He was quick-witted and a past master at taking insults with a grin. He would skin back his gums and show a peckerwood all thirty-six of his big yellow teeth, and the moment the peckerwood turned his back, he'd cut his throat. He had been sentenced to life for raping this piece of white trash and every day the white hacks at the chain gang beat him unconscious for supper. But when he was alone with Tomsson Black at night in the dormitory, he would laugh about it.

"I were goin' through this scrub cotton country 'round Selma and it were so hot my balls were dryin' up and I stopped at this grimy pine shack to beg for a drinka water. From the looks of it, I thought they was niggers livin' there. But a green-eyed white bitch answered the back door. One look at her, I was ready to run my ass off. But 'fore I could get my feet movin' she shot out a skinny hand and grabbed holda me. 'If'n you run, nigger, I gonna scream,' she say.

"Sweat popped out on my head and I felt my asshole tightenin' up. 'I ain't gonna run, lady,' I promise, lookin' out the corners of my eyes. 'I'se jes movin' my feet 'cause y'all's pullin' my dick so hard.' 'Git your ass inside,' she say, pullin' me in by my dick. 'Lady, I just wanna get a drinka water and go,' I say. 'And if you let go my dick, I'll go without no water.' 'You can't go now, nigger, you jes' got here,' she say. 'You gotta fuck me first and if you don't fuck me good, I'm gonna call my old man who's plowing out there in the field and have him come in here and blow your head off.'

"I look through the open window and see a sweat-stained peckerwood plowing a two-mule team not a half-field away. And there was I, didn't have no pistol, no knife, nothing but my raggedy ass and that peckerwood had a shotgun tied to the handle of his plow, like he expected niggers every day. I were so scared I fell down on the floor outa his sight. Then this trash lay down on the floor 'side me and pulled up her skirt and spread her naked legs.

"'Shuck off your pants and gimme that black dick, nigger,' she say. 'Sssshhh, not so loud,' I shushed her, 'cause it looked to me like that peckerwood could hear her from where he was plowing.

"But she jes' raise her head and look out over the window sill and say, 'He can't hear nothin' but them mules fart.'

"Even looking at that white pussy spread out'n front of me, I were so scared I couldn't get a hard-on, but I 'gan fuckin' her with a limber dick to keep her from screamin' until it 'gan hardenin' up. It musta 'gan gettin' good to her for she start twistin' her bare ass on the wooden floor and cryin' every time it got a splinter. And when I start thinkin' of her ass gettin' all splintered up it 'gan gettin' good to me, too, and I start pumpin' my ass up and down like the fly wheel on a locomotive. Her peckerwood husband musta looked up and seen my black ass risin' and fallin' above the window sill, 'cause he call out suddenly, 'What in the world are you doin' with that old automobile tire, Maybelle?' If she had jes' let it go at that, it mighta been all right, but she had to go and say, 'It ain't no automobile tire, I polishin' the stove.'

"He musta stood there and thought about that and it must notta sounded right for all of a sudden he come in through the back door with his shotgun in his hand. He stood there red as a redbird, aiming that gun at me, and I thought for a moment I were a goner. But he took long enough to say, 'I'm gonna blow your brains out, nigger, for rapin' my old lady,' and I knew I were safe. I were so 'lieved I said, 'I weren't rapin' her, boss. I were jes tryna getta drink of water.' And all that peckerwood did was take me into town and have me tried for rape."

Tomsson Black laughed. "You must have been lightly dressed," he observed.

"All I had was my pants coverin' my bare ass," Hoop confessed. "But that taught me. Heresomeafter, I'se always goin' to wear drawers when I go walkin'."

Listening to Hoop, one would think he was amused by the eroticism of white people. But Tomsson Black didn't think it was funny. In his estimation, white people's eroticism was responsible for all lynchings of blacks by whites, and it had done more to alienate the races than all other causes put together. This eroticism had made the whites into liars, cheats, thieves, and hypocrites, and had proved to be more dangerous than their hate. Hoop knew that a black man could handle a nigger-hating cracker, but a nigger-loving crackeress was poison.

Tomsson Black had not always been his name. He had been christened George Washington Lincoln by a father who had a valid predisposition for the names of former presidents, for his own Christian name was Thomas Jonathan Lincoln.

This lineage of black Lincolns had its roots in slavery. The first black Lincoln was the chattel of a cotton planter named Hassan Hardy Hargreaves, who owned a large plantation on the delta of the Mississippi River near Port Gibson. At the time of his birth by the lusty black breeder, Gee, the first thing that met the gaze of the overseer as he looked about for a suitable object to name the newborn slave after was the gray moss hanging from the limbs of a rotting oak. Hence the name Moss. Only the overseer knew the father of the newly-born Moss was a field slave called Haw. Moss never knew who his father was, anymore than a heifer knows what bull it was sired by, nor did he ever feel the need for knowing.

The Hargreaves were a very large family. In addition to seven sons and five daughters, Mrs. Hargreaves's spinster sister and her bedridden mother and Mr. Hargreaves's two orphaned nephews lived with them. They had a very large colonial-style mansion in a park that ran down to the river-bank and more than a thousand slaves to till their fields and do their bidding.

When Moss was considered old enough to work at the age of six he was assigned to help the slave blacksmith, Atlas. The former helper, Piggy, who had become twelve, had been sent to the field to chop and pick cotton. He fanned the forge, collected the horse manure for the roses, and held the horses' reins while Atlas was shoeing them. On occasions when Atlas became too hot, Moss would douse him with water from the bucket used to cool the horseshoes.

Moss had one of his ears bitten off by a recalcitrant mare and several times he was bitten on the face and arms due to his fearlessness with the horses. By the time he was twelve and old enough to be sent to the fields in his turn, he resembled a young black monster. On the very eve of his departure, a horse kicked Atlas in the head, killing him instantly, and Moss found himself elevated to the role of blacksmith. He proved to be a good blacksmith and could control the spirited horses with ease, thanks, as the overseer jokingly put it, to the fear his face inspired in them.

During the Civil War the horses disappeared from the plantation when six of the sons went off to fight in the Confederate Army. A blacksmith was no longer needed and Moss was put in the field. After the war had been in progress for some time, a rumor spread like wildfire among the slaves that they had been freed by a white God called Lincoln, a rumor that turned them from willing workers to recalcitrant ones.

Master Hargreaves suspected that an intinerant peddlar of patent medicines, who had passed by several days earlier, had started this rumor. Although he was suffering from anxiety and yellow jaundice, he got up from his sick bed, had a mule saddled, and tracked the innocent peddlar to a plantation a hundred miles downriver and shot him dead. Still, the rumor persisted and grew into a fact when emissaries of the Union Army canvassed the plantations to tell the slaves that the war was over and they were free.

The blacks did not know what to do with their freedom and many elected to stay on the plantation for their food and shelter. Moss was among the first to leave. It was then that he took the name of Lincoln, since it was the only name he knew with the exception of "Bible" that had no association with slavery. As Moss Lincoln wandered through the hostile South of the Reconstruction Era, he survived only through his fleetness of foot, his ability to digest acorns, and his grotesque appearance, which got him odd jobs as the "wild man" at local fairs.

Because he could not read, write, or count above ten, he did not know his age. Moss was thirty-three years old when he left the plantation a free man. Two years later he met a slave girl when he sneaked up to a kitchen door of a sleeping manor house early one morning to beg food from the cook.

She was alarmed by the sight of him, for she thought he was a runaway slave. He looked as though he had been severely punished for running away before. It was three years since the Civil War had ended, but she still didn't know the slaves were free.

He hung about the plantation all day and saw her again that night. By morning they were lovers and he had convinced her that they were free. Tying all of her belongings into a bandana handkerchief, she left the plantation with him before daybreak. Her name was Pan. Thus began the lineage of the black Lincolns.

Having a wife saved Moss's life several times as they walked across Mississippi toward Tennessee, which they thought was "up North" where Lincoln was a god. By then, the Ku Klux Klan was the scourge of dark country roads and single black males without a white "protector" were apt to be hung outright.

They arrived in Memphis in the spring of 1869 and were surprised to find an already-established ghetto of freed slaves, all fighting amongst themselves for existence. Thanks to his muscular physique and ferocious appearance, Moss survived. He got a job as a blacksmith's helper at a livery stable owned by whites in the business section of Memphis. However, he and his wife had to live in the black shantytown under conditions infinitely worse than those of the horses he helped to shoe.

Pan's first three babies were still-born due to a vitamin deficiency caused by a diet of fat meat and home-made corn grits. Finally a male baby lived and the exultant father asked Mr. MacDowell, his blacksmith boss, to give him a name. MacDowell, without an instant's thought, said, "Zachary. The poor bugger's gotta be rough'n ready to survive in that poisonous swamp where you niggers live."

Four other male babies were born to Pan and were named in turn by the amiable Mr. MacDowell John Quincey, William Henry, Julius Augustus, Caius, and Napoleon. Unfortunately, all but Zachary died—one from Yellow Fever, one from pellagra, one choked to death on a pork bone, and the other was killed by a mad dog that found its way into their shanty. Whether they died because of the brave names Mr. MacDowell had given them, or in spite of them, the illiterate, superstitious ex-slave and his suspicious wife never decided, but they agreed to name the next one all by themselves. Unfortunately, there were no others.

Zachary grew up their only child and, in his turn, became a blacksmith, going to work for the same livery stable as his father when Moss died. Zachary married the third daughter of the black preacher who had a church of an unnamed denomination in a rotting, abandoned warehouse on the lower end of Beale Street, where it runs into the Mississippi.

At that time, Beale Street was occupied almost exclusively by white trash who were scarcely better off than the ex-slaves, and Preacher Gus was considered a formidable man for daring to preach there. Preacher Gus was a veritable Hercules who, on his regular job, easily carried the five-hundred pound bales of cotton on his back from the warehouses down to the pier where they were loaded aboard river boats bound for New Orleans. It was considered equally daring of Zachary to marry one of Gus's grown daughters, since it was rumored that Gus wanted them all for himself.

Their first son was born in 1912 and Mr. MacDowell, by then a doddering old man but still official blacksmith of the Main Street Livery Stable, promptly suggested the name of Thomas Jonathan (Stonewall). Zachary's wife, Lucy, could not only read and write, but she had attended a boarding school in Nashville called Fisk Institute, and she knew enough about America's history to know that the name was that of a Confederate Army General who had died in the Civil War defending slavery. She did not think it an appropriate name for a black child, the grandson of slaves.

However, Zachary contended that Mr. MacDowell would be angry if they didn't use the name and might very likely fire him. She relented, but would never call her son anything but Jonathan.

Lucy bore three daughters afterward, but in 1917 Zachary was drafted into the U. S. Army, in spite of his being the head and sole provider of a large family. The expeditionary force on its way to France to fight the Hun was desperately in need of blacksmiths to serve both the cavalry and artillery. Unfortunately, Zachary, a non-combatant, was killed by enemy artillery during the Battle-on-the-Marne while his company was being moved from one position to another. Lucy and her four young children were left without a husband and father.

Lucy took her children to live with her aging father, Preacher Gus, who was by then a widower himself. He welcomed back his daughter to cook and clean for him, since all of his other children had left the roost. But Lucy was still young, only twenty-eight, and she had no intention of being her father's housekeeper and nurse during his declining years. She was educated and still lovely, rare in a black woman of that time, living as she did in the Memphis slums of Beale Street. In spite of her four children, there was no shortage of suitors for her hand.

She chose a dock worker in the image of her father, a huge, brawny black who could neither read nor write, to the consternation of other suitors who had lighter skin and better educations. To her intimate women friends, she confessed that she didn't want to take a book to bed and wanted to see her husband naked on white sheets.

His name was Ralph Sherwin and he adored her, but he didn't care too much for her children since he wanted children of his own. The children sensed they were unwanted and, even at their tender ages, began to drift away. Jonathan was eight and the only one attending the jerry-built wooden elementary school that Memphis provided for black children. Shortly he began to play hookey and ended up sweeping the floor and racking balls for a new pool room on Beale Street. The blues were coming into vogue at that time, and often he'd stay out all night hiding in the shadows of some popular gin joint to hear them played and sung.

His two eldest sisters, six and seven years of age, went to live with aunts and eventually became prostitutes. His baby sister, who had only been three when his mother married again, had been accepted by Ralph as a child of his own. During the ensuing thirteen years she was provided with eleven half-brothers and sisters.

"Johnny," as Jonathan was known, turned out to be a ne'er do well. One night he met a light-complexioned, teen-aged girl trying to hustle in a gin joint. He took her home with the intention of becoming her pimp. Two days later, when he was trying to place her in a house run by a tall, raw-boned black woman with a scarred face, he ran into his two sisters who were working there. This shocked him out of his intention. Instead, he married the girl, whose name was Naomi, and got her a job as a laundress and chamber-maid for a white family. He shortly joined the domestic staff as a gardner and handyman in self defense so that he could keep his wife faithful.

When they began to raise a family, their employers gave them the use of a tumble-down cottage that had housed an overseer during slavery. By 1942, five years after their marriage, they had four brown tots, who were called "those Lincoln pickaninnies" by the white family.

In April of 1942, Thomas Jonathan Lincoln was inducted into the U. S. Army as a private in the infantry. Until then,

Jonathan had accepted Jim Crow and segregation as the normal way of life. He did his basic training in Southern Jim Crow camps. In December of that year he was sent to the Pacific Theater and spent the next eleven months in a company of other black laborers building and cleaning out latrines for white servicemen on the Pacific Islands.

During that time he smelled and shoveled so much white shit, not to mention the amount of shit he had to take from the whites, that he developed an intense hatred for all white people. Before then he had never actively hated white people. They lived in a white world and he lived in his black world, dependant on them, serving them, but always indulged by them in the special fashion that white Southerners showed toward their good niggers. But the whites in the army didn't make any allowances for his being black. They worked him like a nigger and treated him like a nigger with no compensating indulgences.

He chopped off the first two fingers of his left hand in order to get discharged. He was discharged, but dishonorably, without any G. I. or other compensating benefits, and his commanding officer told him he was lucky not to have been imprisoned.

He arrived back in Memphis, broke and discharged, to learn that the news of his dishonor had arrived ahead of him. His wife had quit her job and gone off with another man, taking their children with her. His former employers were infuriated both by his wife's desertion from their employ and by his own disloyalty to his country. They would have nothing to do with him.

No one would lend him any money and a white deputy from the Sheriff's Office suggested that he leave town. In desperation, with no money or possessions but his ragged uniform, he hitchhiked to St. Louis. The only people who gave him lifts were, as was to be expected, black. He always stepped off the road when a white motorist came into view if he saw him in time.

He immediately discovered that during the war against Japan, St. Louis was no place for an unemployed and friendless black man with a dishonorable discharge from the army. He moved into the suburban University City, using his instinct to lead him to the estates of wealthy whites. He knew they would be short of help and unconcerned about his dishonorable discharge. Secretly, many wealthy and intelligent whites saw no disgrace in a black man getting out of the Jim Crow army by whatever means possible. Plus, he was strong enough and sound enough to do all the chores they could find, despite the missing fingers that scarcely incapacitated him at all.

He got a room on credit in the shanty of a black widow employed as cook and housekeeper by one of the white families in the lovely little town and whose only time off was every Thursday afternoon and evening and every second Sunday afternoon. Mrs. Booker's four-room shanty was in the shantytown for black servants located in the swampland along the southern bank of the Missouri River, on the outskirts of University City.

Mrs. Booker didn't have time to live in it herself, since most of the black servant women lived in now, and didn't need any outside accomodations since all the able-bodied men were away. Only the aged and the infirm black men were about, and Mrs. Booker didn't want any of them as roomers. What she wanted was someone as strong and willing—not to mention eager—as she was herself. It was true that Jonathan had a couple of fingers missing, but he didn't seem to be missing anything otherwise, so Mrs. Booker let him have the room on credit, trusting him to be there when she was to pay off his bill.

Much to Mrs. Booker's disappointment, however, it didn't turn out that way at all. On his first visit to one of University City's small estates, Jonathan got a day's employment as a much-needed handyman and carpenter, the only occupations for which he was qualified. Soon he was working every day on different estates as a handyman and gardener and when Mrs. Booker finally got her Thursday off, all she found at home was a week's rent and the word "thanks."

Jonathan discovered that the residents of University City were much in need of his services. He didn't need any tools because each estate had its own. He didn't need any food for at each estate he found a black cook eager to feed him. He did not lack for sexual fulfillment for there were scores of black women to fulfill his every desire. He had no competition, since every able-bodied black man was either in the armed forces or else out of sight.

By the end of 1944, Jonathan found that he was prosperous. And he was in love. For two months he had been sleeping with a lovely black nineteen-year-old chambermaid. When she told him that she was pregnant during the second week of January, 1945, he confessed that he was married but that his wife had run off with another man.

"Well, what's stopping you from marrying me, then?" she asked. "You know these white folks aren't going to care if she don't raise no stink."

So at the end of the month he married Hattie Bourchard and at the beginning of March they set up housekeeping on the top floor of a decaying carriage house on a run-down, neglected estate near the southwest corner of town where the Missouri River empties into the Mississippi. The estate was owned by two spinster sisters in their sixties, who were among the last descendants of a tycoon who had built one of the western railroad empires, Major George Mortimer Purcell. In Major Purcell's day it was used as a summer house. The manor house was a sixty-three room castle faced with brown stone and garnished with many stained-glass leaded windows. It had three octagonal towers, each comprising a single large room with eight picture windows that overlooked the estate.

Surrounding the castle was the "green," a velvet-smooth lawn of circular shape. From the drawing room windows, the lawn sloped down to a marble fountain large enough to serve as a swimming pool, beyond which was a rose arbor the size of a plantation laid out between seried rows of white marble columns on brown granite pedestals. Surrounding all of this was a park that served as Major Purcell's private hunting preserve.

But the upkeep of such a place was very expensive and it couldn't be sold since no one who could afford it wanted it. As a consequence, Major Purcell's heirs simply abandoned it and eventually the Wharton sisters, Major Purcell's grandnieces, settled there to die. By this time the estate was in a hopeless state of decay. The lawn and rose garden were overgrown with weeds and poison ivy, rutted by gopher holes and soil erosion so far advanced that it was beyond reclamation. The park had reverted into a riverbank jungle and the furnishings of the house were slowly disintegrating from rot, mildew, and the continuous assaults of voracious insects.

The Wharton sisters lived in a small apartment at the back of their house. Their one servant, an old and toothless black hag scarcely worth her keep, slept in the old-fashioned kitchen that was big enough to serve an army.

When the black Lincolns approached them about a place to stay in that big empty castle or one of its outbuildings, the Whartons seized the opportunity. The two old women welcomed the protection to be afforded by having a man about the place, even a black one, although they had been without such protection since they had moved in during the early years of the Great Depression. They realized that he could clear the weeds from the driveway and fix the rattling windows, but declined to have him live under the roof with them, even though that roof covered sixty empty rooms. They rented to him the three empty rooms over an old, unused, scorpion-infested carriage house for fifteen dollars a month, plus doing small chores for them.

This arrangement suited the Lincolns fine. Hattie had become calling him Tom because his first wife had called him Johnny. Since a bus into University City stopped at the foot of the driveway every hour, Tom was able to get back and forth to his jobs in the city and Hattie was able to shop, cook, and keep house for him. Unfortunately, it didn't work out quite the way they'd planned. The Wharton sisters demanded so much from both of them whenever they were at home that Hattie went back to work as a free-lance maid and laundress. She and Tom made it a practice thereafter to stay at their jobs until it was too dark for the Whartons to call upon their services.

It was in that vine-covered carriage house that they shared with hundreds of lizards that their first child was born on August 29th, 1945. Thomas Jonathan Lincoln insisted, over the protests of Hattie, who wished to name him Frederick Douglass Lincoln, that he be named George Washington Lincoln. Tom hated white people but he couldn't do without them and he knew they were instinctively flattered by the fact that more black children were named after George Washington, who kept black slaves, because he was the "father" of the country, than after Abraham Lincoln, who had freed the slaves.

Little George Washington Lincoln owed the nickname Tomsson Black to his schoolmates. The boy was extremely defensive because his mother washed and cooked at Poro College. His fellow students wrongly charged that his father did anything the Misses Wharton wished, and called him an Uncle Tom's son. Young Tomsson fought many a battle to defend his father's honor, but the name clung to him. Finally, he decided to keep it.

Indeed, he eventually came to be liked and admired in the black community because of the courage he displayed in every circumstance. When he confronted gangs of white youths and was given the choice of fighting or running away, he was psychologically predisposed to fight. He had always been tall, strong, and athletic for his years, perhaps because he had eaten vast quantities of chitterlings, something his father fancied as much as beer.

At Wendell Phillips High School, he was allowed to join the basketball and baseball teams and to run the hundred yard hurdles. He learned the art of boxing at the black YMCA and taught himself how to ski and skate in the mountains.

Tomsson Black was about to graduate when his father was shot and killed by an angry white man in a tavern. Insane with rage, the youngster nearly beat to death a white police detective who had come to their home to investigate. He was forced to leave town quickly in order to escape punishment.

He went to Oakland, California, where a friend of his father's was running a nightclub on Seventh Street. For a while, he washed dishes there in order to make a living, then became a waiter in a white boarding school on Telegraph Street in Berkeley, near the University of California campus. He was admitted to the university because of his sports prowess and eventually became a football star and political science graduate. At approximately the same time, he encountered a few Black Panthers in Oakland and joined the organization.

Cutting a splendid figure in his black leather beret and jacket, he became a popular member of the group. However, he found the Panthers badly organized and poorly trained in the basics of self defense.

He decided to form his own organization, which he named The Big Blacks. During a meeting in a warehouse on the outskirts of Oakland, a militant who was standing watch at the entrance to their headquarters was gunned down by police officers. In a flash of inspiration, Tomsson Black ran outside as he heard the gunfire and took photographs of the dying black man and the white policemen standing over him with their guns in their hands. The photos were proof that the dead man was not armed, although the police insisted that he had drawn his gun first. Tomsson Black charged the police with assassinating a defenseless man and the American press made much of the case.

At that stage in his life, Tomsson Black became attracted to Marxist ideology and began a series of tours to different communist countries. Strangely enough, the Department of State neither tried to prevent his visits to these countries nor bothered to investigate him upon his return.

CHAPTER 12

It was obvious that Tomsson Black was a much younger man than Hoop because he had never learned the simple facts of life. Nor had Tomsson Black accepted the realities of his two-faced environment; he had not acquired the stoicism that a black man needs to survive in the modern world. Nor had he learned the art of bald-faced hypocrisy that is so important in life. Tomsson Black was an innocent, still believing that whites could be honest, fair, decent, and just, even though they weren't. He still believed they could make the right choice. There were many other blacks who shared his belief.

He was still so furious with the white woman who had sent him to prison for rape that he couldn't bear to talk about her. He wasn't like Hoop. He couldn't stand to admit why he had raped her. He felt dirtied by her action as though she had covered him with her shit. He was both humiliated and outraged at once. He hadn't forgiven her nor her hypocrite husband. He didn't think getting life imprisonment for what he had done was funny. He promised himself that if he ever got out of prison and found them still alive anywhere on the planet Earth, he was going to cut their white throats to the bone.

It was these thoughts that gave him such a look of perpetual anger. Still, he was careful to be studiously well-behaved. Partly because of his good behavior, and partly because the white woman he had raped had been from the North, the Southern white-trash hacks didn't abuse him. Served her right, they thought, having a nigger on the same boat. Tomsson Black often had the same thought himself—in reverse—served his own ass right for being on the same boat with the teasing, nigger-happy whore.

But strangely enough, it had been inevitable. He had been heading for that white slut's cunt all his life, although he hadn't realized it. He had just moved in that direction faster during the previous year.

He had returned to the U. S. from his highly-publicized world travels in communist countries, where he had acquainted himself with modern revolutionary ideologies and the latest techniques and tactics for planning and executing guerilla warfare, and had found the American State Department reluctant to penalize him. However, he discovered the reason for this was the State Department's understanding that blacks were both psychologically and emotionally incapable of organizing and conducting a coordinated action under the command of a single leader.

What he had known all along had just been further substantiated. Blacks were more individualistic than whites.

Too many of them desired to be leaders and too few were willing to serve in the ranks. The knowledge dispirited him. He began to lose hope. He concluded that if blacks wouldn't organize, they'd always remain vulnerable to the whites, they'd always be pissed on by whites, and forever remain second-class citizens.

It was then, as both escape and therapy, that he had begun moving in the circles of Northern white liberals who needed the presence of a black face to prove their liberalism. A single dark face in their company had more social value than a thousand proclamations of racial brotherhood. What was more, black skin titilated the sexual inclinations of whites and incited their eroticism. One look at a black face fanned white desire into every imaginable shape and fantasy, frontside up and backside up, forepart behind and hindpart before, upside down and downside up, coming and going and standing still, in a ball, in a chain, in the air, on the ground, under water, and in the mind.

White women had propositioned Tomsson Black in every way under the sun, so it wasn't naivete that allowed him to be persuaded into going on a cruise in the Gulf of Mexico on the yacht of a liberal, white millionaire philanthropist named Edward Tudor Goodfeller, III. Eddie Goodfeller had told Tomsson Black that he was descended from the General Goodfeller who commanded the English redcoats fighting against George Washington at the battle of Valley Forge, and he had a painting of a red-coated general astride a white horse hanging in his stateroom to prove it.

Tomsson Black grinned and told him he believed it. Eddy Goodfeller patted him on the back and said, "Good boy." Tomsson Black didn't let it affect their friendship because he knew that all Goodfeller wanted was to be loved and admired, especially by blacks and other inferiors, as do all American whites. He wasn't even provoked when Goodfeller told him that one of his ancestors had owned a larger number of slaves than any other single individual, and that this ancestor's success in the rum trade was the origin of the Goodfeller fortune. Tomsson Black said that maybe Goodfeller's ancestor had owned his ancestors, for one of his ancestors had been the champion sugarcane cutter of all the slaves in the South. Goodfeller grinned embarrassedly and patted him on the back. "Have a rum and coke," he invited. "And I assure you this rum wasn't made by my ancestor from the sugarcane cut by your ancestor."

"All the pity," Tomsson Black had replied. "It would have been some damn good rum."

Edward T. Goodfeller was a robust, ruddy-faced man in his mid-forties. He had wide shoulders, was of medium height, and had a shock of white hair that looked electric. His ruddiness was due more to weather than drink, and his piercing blue eyes were those of a sailor. Only people who were envious and malicious had ever called him a homosexual, for he was the very epitome of robust vitality, virility, and heterosexuality and had a beautiful young wife to prove it.

His yacht, a schooner of almost two hundred feet in

length, was powered by diesel engines, but also had three masts for sailing. It had a crew of twelve and could accomodate an additional twelve passengers. Goodfeller was very proud of it. On this particular trip, there were only eight passengers, including Goodfeller and his wife. Although the trip was purportedly a fishing expedition, it had quickly degenerated into drinking and mate-swapping. All were couples except Tomsson Black and his cabin-mate, a very courteous and correct young white college student, whom Tomsson Black seldom saw. He wondered amusedly if Goodfeller thought he was a homosexual.

Such was definitely not the case with Goodfeller's wife. From the very first, she had put herself out to madden him with her white body. It was the first time she'd had a black man all to herself and she intended to make the most of it. Her husband wouldn't have thought of keeping tabs on her and the other white wives respected her claim and kept to themselves.

Her name was Barbara, but friends called her Babs. She was almost a dead ringer for Cotton Tail Harrison—the same type of corn-silk blonde with big innocent-looking blue eyes that gave the impression that butter wouldn't melt in her mouth, along with a figure that would make a preacher ball the jack. She didn't need any birth control pills—she was safe, a factor that allowed her to indulge in any depravity that struck her fancy.

Goodfeller indulged her as far as it was possible; he kept

out of her way. So they went their separate ways as far as sexual fulfillment was concerned.

When she first saw this tall, handsome young black, nearly bursting out of his swim trunks, she became frantic to seduce him. But it didn't happen. Tomsson Black kept himself to himself.

He and the other single man had a choice cabin adjoining the Goodfellers' suite, which gave Babs a greater opportunity to spin her web. She spent a great deal of time alone in her bedroom walking about stark naked with the passage door open, waiting for Tomsson Black to pass.

But when her opportunity finally arrived, and she had shaken her white ass tantalizingly at him, he got the message. The message had said "keep away from this screwball or you'll be wearing stripes and they won't be pinstripes from London."

His seemingly cavalier rejection of her provocative invitation outraged her. Who did this black nigger think he was? A white homosexual? But maybe he was just scared, she reassured herself. She had heard that niggers were scared of naked white women, or at least when they first saw them. She had heard of niggers bursting out in hysterical laughter at their first sight of a white woman's pussy.

But she vowed to get this beautiful black, if it was the last thing she ever did. She waylaid him in the bar, at meals, at dances. Her husband and the other whites stood aside and watched her campaign, not one of them ever doubting the final outcome.

Tomsson Black avoided her as best he could, but he couldn't ignore her entirely. She was his host's wife and he was the lion of the entourage—black lion, true enough, but of the African species, nevertheless.

She insinuated herself into his thoughts until he had nightmares of her white legs spread above him like the Colussus of Rhodes, spurting molten metal that shrivelled his penis into a charred and stinking cinder. He'd wake up screaming, frightening the wits out of his courteous young white cabin mate.

The next time he passed Barbara's bedroom and found her revealing all her alluring white nudity through the open passage door, he wheeled into the room and slammed shut the door.

"You slut," he roared, beside himself with rage as he tore the buttons from his fly. "You dirty teaser, you vicious jail-bait, I'm gonna strangle you with it and see how you like it." His black face knotted with fury, and his muscles quivered from the violence of passion.

She shuddered with ecstasy as though each epithet lashed her with erotic passion. But when he tried to force himself into her, she held him off. He then tried to pull away, but she wouldn't let him go. Suddenly, as in her dreams, thick, sticky semen was spurting over her naked legs. All the glands of her body opened and released a flood like lava from an erupting volcano. She gave a loud moaning cry of such ecstasy that he hit her in the face.

"Ohhh, beat me, my beautiful black nigger! Beat me and rape me!" she cried.

He was so enraged he kept hitting her in the face until he felt another erection coming on and plunged it so viciously into her that it seemed he wanted to split her apart.

Blood was running from her nostrils and from the corners of her eyes, which had already swollen shut and were beginning to turn black. Her face rapidly ballooned out and began turning all the colors of the rainbow. Even then she was consumed with a passion so intense they both came together in an effluvium of hate and ecstasy.

At that moment Goodfeller walked into the room. "Well, well," he cried jovially. "Success at last." But when he saw her face he stammered stupidly, "W-w-what happened?"

She pushed Tomsson Black off of her and said, "This black nigger beat me and raped me. Get the doctor and have this black bastard put in irons."

"I can't do that," he said, but he telephoned for the doctor nevertheless.

"You'd better," she threatened. "He'd better be locked up before the doctor gets here and sees me like this."

Ignoring her, Goodfeller looked at Tomsson Black accusingly. "You didn't have to beat her."

"What the hell do you know about it?" Tomsson Black raved. "There's nothing you can do with a slut like this

but beat her. Not if you're trapped. Not if you're black."
Goodfeller nodded understandingly. "I know, I know. But
you've got yourself in trouble. Now you go to your cabin
and lock yourself in and don't discuss this with anyone and
I'll do my best to save you."

"You sissie louse," Babs lisped through her swollen mouth.
"If you don't have this black animal locked up this instant
I'm going to tell everyone on board about him beating me
and raping me and you taking his side."

"Babs, let's not be hasty—" he began, but at that moment
the doctor knocked on the door and the decision was taken
out of his hands.

The ship's doctor was a thin, ascetic, middle-aged pur-
itan from Newport, where Goodfeller kept his ship berthed,
who had a very low tolerance for black people. He gave
his services free as the ship's doctor on some of Goodfeller's southern cruises in exchange for his keep. But he
had always viewed the sexual promiscuity aboard ship,
even when limited to white husbands and wives who were
guests, with tremendous disapproval. He had felt shocked
and outraged from the very beginning of this cruise by the
appearance of a black man among the guests. Now this final
disaster was no more than he had expected. He took but
one glance at the bruised and battered face of the nude
white woman, then leveled his gaze threatening on the
guilty black. From then on, Tomsson Black knew his fate
was sealed.

Because the ship was in the territorial waters of the state of Alabama, Tomsson Black was taken into custody and tried in that state. Life imprisonment was mandatory for a black man convicted of raping a white woman there. It was a foregone conclusion that once Mrs. Barbara Goodfeller took the stand and pointed out Tomsson Black as her assailant, it was bye-bye blackbird.

She looked him straight in the eye as she described in a loud, clear voice and in graphic detail how he had beaten and raped her, down to the pain of the last blow he had rained upon her face. And when she related her most intimate feelings at the time he had penetrated her, she blushed bright red, as did every other white woman in the courthouse, in sympathy.

When he was sentenced to life imprisonment, Tomsson Black's sex dried up like a plant cut off at the root. However, it was reported that Goodfeller went down into niggertown that night and tried to atone. Afterwards he accused his wife of being a depraved, heartless slut, without honor or morals or even common decency. He accused her of being more callous than any slave-owner's wife or daughter, more monstrous than any of the Gorgon sisters. He could not find the vocabulary to express the full hatred and contempt he felt for her.

But three years later, when she had a change of heart and forced him to spend one hundred thousand dollars to secure for Tomsson Black a full pardon with restoration of citizenship, the hatred and contempt he had felt for her he now turned on the niggers. He came to hate niggers with an intensity only matched by a former nigger-loving liberal. He hated them because their very existence threatened him with exposure as an inhibited white "mother" for scores of black homosexuals.

CHAPTER 13

Tomsson Black was thirty-two years old when he got out of prison. He was six feet, two inches tall, with the bold, heavy features and coarse, straight, jet-black hair of a red Indian, but his eyes were a spectacular shade of brown. His complexion was the hot black of soft coal just beginning to burn, his mouth was wide and shaped for laughter, and his thick, full lips which were several shades lighter than his skin, gave the impression of great passion. All women wanted to be kissed by such lips. When he smiled, which was seldom since he had left prison, his brilliant white teeth lit up his whole black face like a beacon in the night. Tomsson Black had always been handsome, now the premature gray at his temples gave him a look of distinction.

He looked considerably older than his thirty-two years, but that was to be expected after his three years on a southern chain gang. But he comported himself with such dignity and gravity he immediately impressed people with his reliability. From prison he went directly to New York and checked into the Pierre Hotel. His distinguished and reliable appearance was such that he was not requested to pay for his room in advance, as was the general policy toward blacks. Despite his cheap clothing and rough edges, he looked like a man of consequence.

The first thing he did was telephone Barbara Goodfeller and ask her to come to the Pierre and visit him. She was both astounded and impressed by his choice of hotel, but she was more intrigued by the thought that he still desired her. For three long years she had believed this lustful compulsion was hers alone, and it stirred her with excitement to think that he desired her, too. She was enthralled by the thought that his three years of enforced celibacy had left him frantic, and her anticipation was so intense that she gave herself the most thorough make-up ever. However, she took so long a time in her preparations to seduce him that when she finally arrived, she found him simmering with rage.

"I ought to beat you," he greeted her. "You haven't changed; still arrogant and tantalizing. Besides which, you'll probably like it so much you'll have me sent back to prison."

"I'll never let you get away from me again," she vowed, embracing him, hoping he would smell her.

He smelled her all right, she smelled just right, like expensive perfume of rich, white, hot cunt, and money.

"Baby, I need money more than love," he said appealingly. "I need a lot of money because what I've got in mind is going to cost a hell of a lot of it."

She was disappointed but not defeated. "I'll give you all the money you want. All I want is you," she added honestly.

"You don't have the kind of money I need, baby," he said.

"But I'll take what you got, then go look for some more from someone else."

"I'll make you rich," she promised.

"Take off your clothes," he ordered.

Quick as a flash she undressed and lay on the bed, her milk-white body glowing with lust. He stripped naked and lay on her, his body like a hand-carved black fetish resting on the whitest silk. She clutched him lovingly, moaning in ecstasy and had an orgasm even before he penetrated her.

He looked down on her indulgently, knowing that he had it made. "Isn't this groovy?"

She smiled and said, "It'll keep me young and beautiful."

Amusedly, he thought that all he had to do to please her was be black enough and big enough.

After they had finished again, she mused, "If slavery still existed, I'd buy you."

"You don't need the institution of slavery," he said. "Just buy me and I'll be your slave forever."

She smiled complacently; she believed him.

Before taking a shower and dressing, she sat at the writing desk and filled out a check for twenty-five thousand dollars which she presented to him.

"Is that enough for my big handsome bull?"

"For this your bull will always keep you in milk," he promised, carefully scrutinizing the check.

"Not my milk, your milk," she corrected.

They found themselves laughing simultaneously.

CHAPTER 14

The massacre on Eighth Avenue released a deluge of horror in the white community. Whites were so shocked and horrified by the actions of their own white law enforcement officers, that they completely ignored the fact that five of them had been killed first by a black maniac. White people were so predisposed to the emotion of guilt, that they were blind to the murderous assault of the homicidal black, and assumed the role of murderer, themselves. They were plunged into a guilty bereavement, and were impregnable to objective reason.

The white community sprinkled its blonde head with ashes and wrapped its shuddering white limbs in sack cloth. It wallowed in a mud bath of remorse. It indulged in an orgy of expiation. The desire to atone became physical. To expiate for its sense of guilt, not only was the white community willing to sacrifice its women, but anxious; and not only were its women willing to be sacrificed, they were avid. Even the most moral of white women were convinced of the palliative qualities of their sex.

Others were more practical-minded. Knowledgeable committees provided means for white donors to give blood to compensate for the blood the black victims lost in death. So much blood was collected that the committee had no place for it and didn't know what to do with it. Someone suggested that they make blood pudding, but this was considered an offensive suggestion. Nevertheless, the donors felt temporarily relieved, almost as though they had masturbated.

And there were some whites who went about crying publically, like citizens did the time F. D. Roosevelt died, touching blacks on the street as if to express their suffering through contact, and sobbingly confessing their sorrow and begging the blacks' forgiveness. There were a few extremists who even bent over and offered their asses for blacks to kick, but blacks weren't sure whether they were meant to kick them or kiss them, so in their traditional manner, they cautiously avoided making any decision at all.

Never had the white community been so passionately consumed with masochistic desire. Nothing would satisfy the whites other than suffering pain at the hands of blacks. They begged blacks to curse them, to strike them, to spit on them, to rape them, and reveled in ecstasy while they were beaten and defiled.

Never had the white community projected such mawkish feelings of guilt. White men, crying unrestrainedly, confessed to deeds and emotions they had kept concealed and had denied for centuries. They were heard to confess to beating blacks, oppressing blacks, corrupting blacks, lusting after blacks, and most violently of all, to hating blacks. Middle-aged, intelligent, prosperous, highly-placed white men confessed to having hated black men all of their lives. No doubt some of this was due to alcohol, which the whites are known to consume as an analgesia against guilt. But of course, this made it no less true. And they confessed that they were indeed devils, as certain discredited blacks had contended all along, and declared that they should be punished for their wickedness. And strangely enough, during this period of compulsive confession, it was reported that a white man had been seen beating himself in The Village, but this was not taken seriously for white men had been seen beating themselves in The Village for many years, and some had even been arrested for indecent exposure.

A group funeral for all the dead blacks was held in a church in Harlem, and was attended by the mayor, the governor, the vice-president, many congressmen, and any number of prominent whites from industry and commerce. A white millionaire was seen chauffeuring his black chauffeur for the occasion and it was said that his wife washed the dishes for their black cook that same evening.

Newspapers were bordered in black that day, and public institutions were draped in black. The American flag in front of the United Nations building was flown at half mast for the day, and the windows of Fifth Avenue department stores displayed lone wreaths of white lillies on black bunting. White men throughout the city wore black shirts in concession to mourning, and white women wore black diamonds.

White ministers conducted concurrent funeral services in all the city's white churches, and their churches were packed with weeping whites who joined in prayer for the souls of the dead blacks. At the same time, memorial services were being conducted on all the television and radio stations of the nation.

The citizens of other nations in the world found it difficult to reconcile this excessive display of guilt by America's white community with its traditional treatment of blacks. What the citizens of the world didn't understand was that American whites are a traditionally masochistic people, and their sense of guilt toward their blacks is an integral part of the national character. ʷˢˢᵒⁿ ²ᵍᵘᵉ - ᴾᵃᵗᵗᵉʳⁿ ᴿʰᵉᵗᵒʳⁱᶜ

However, the official inquiry was conducted by officials whose normal duty is was to prevent blacks from opposing their oppression. The committee, appointed by the mayor, consisted of the police commissioner, the district attorney, the medical examiner, and a black politician who was president of the city council. It was their duty to investigate the incidents leading up to the massacre, and determine whether there was cause for the offenders to be punished.

To protect the white cops involved from hysterical members of the white community, they were locked in the cells of the homicide bureau, attached to the district attorney's office in the court house. After they were made safe from their public, the committee was then free to inquire into the causes and effects of the massacre.

It was learned that the root cause had been a black man armed with an automatic rifle of high calibre who had launched himself upon a course of killing as many white cops as possible. His motivation for such anti-social, homicidal behavior was still to be ascertained, but they admitted among themselves that the urge to kill white cops had been growing in the black community in recent years. A psychiatrist was consulted as the first expert. He testified that in his opinion, such homicidal compulsions in American blacks were easily understandable in the framework of the existing structure of American society—in fact it was inevitable. Blacks had always considered white police as their major enemy. He was surprised that there were so few incidents of this nature. The committee decided to drop that line of inquiry.

The district attorney then took over the questioning, as was his perogative. The police commissioner, being the expert, took over the answering.

Q: What did this black actually do?

A: The black man stood in a front window of a tenement on Eighth Avenue in Harlem and shot two innocent policemen who were peacefully patrolling the street in a police cruiser. He shot them without warning or for any reason which has yet been discovered. And when other policemen in cruisers came to place him under arrest, he shot three of them dead, wounded seven, then held them off with his high-powered automatic rifle until a police tank was sent to their assistance.

Q: Where were the blacks—as opposed to the participants in the gun battle—until the massacre took place?

A: They were lying on the floor of the entrance hall.

Q: Didn't they feel safe there?

A: Evidently not.

Q: And where were the accused officers?

A: They had taken cover beneath the police cruisers in the street.

Q: That arrangement seems to me to be peaceful enough. How, then, did the blacks get themselves shot?

A: Suddenly they rushed out into the street.

Q: And the officers shot them for that?

A: Well, in view of what had already happened to them, being attacked by the black maniac with the rifle, and already having three of their number killed and several others wounded, they thought the blacks were attacking them. They had come out shouting and screaming like savages on the war path with their faces daubed with white paint—

Q: Paint?

A: Well, it turned out afterwards to be plaster dust, but in the stress and excitement of the gun battle, they couldn't be expected to notice that.

Q: And they shot them in self defense?

A: They thought they were shooting in self defense. And then again, the black killer with the rifle hadn't been seen since the first cannon shot and they weren't sure but what they were covering his escape.

Q: Yes, yes, we can understand that. But what caused the blacks to rush suddenly into the street when they had felt safe, and in fact had been safe, in the shelter of the entrance hall?

A: It's hard to say. It's like cattle stampeding. Some minor incident, a sound, a flash of reflected sunlight from a shard of mirror, panics the entire herd and they rush in pell-mell flight to their doom.

"You should have been a poet, sir," the district attorney observed, smiling.

Experts from the appropriate departments presented the statistics of the damage:

Five police officers killed, seven wounded.

Nineteen police cars damaged to varying extents.

Fifty-nine blacks killed, thirteen wounded.

One tenement building completely destroyed by cannon fire, the two adjacent buildings damaged beyond immediate occupancy.

An estimated five-hundred people—between fifty and one hundred families—made homeless.

Those made homeless detained in a hastily constructed stockade in Upper Central Park.

The committee of inquiry ordered that the detainees be interrogated.

It was discovered that not one of them had ever seen or heard of the black man who had killed the white cops. He had never been seen about the building, coming or going, in the tenement flat, on the street, in the window; it was as though he had sprung full-grown from the walls of the tenement with a rifle in his hand.

No one had the slightest idea why he would suddenly attack and kill white policemen, who had always been good and kind to black people. They could not imagine him doing a thing like that; none of them would even think of killing a kindly white cop. Not one of them had seen him fire at the patrol car or at any of the other police cars that appeared subsequently. None of them knew anything, had seen anything, had heard anything, or said anything of importance. It was as though they had spent that night on another planet.

irony of masking

The police laboratory identified the gun as identical to the gun which had figured in the murder of the black woman and the accidental death of the black man which had occurred ten days previous and less than five minutes walking distance from where the massacre had taken place. The gun, almost damanged beyond identity by the cannon blast, held no clues, except for one fingerprint from the black killer, recorded from the fragment of a finger which had been recovered from the debris.

THE MYSTERY GUN, the press called it.

At first a faint chill of uneasiness affected the white community by the thought of mystery guns falling into the hands of homicidal blacks.

Then the uneasiness grew as the press published detailed reports of the wanton killing of five white policemen by the black killer. Visions stirred in the minds of white citizens of blacks running amok with mystery guns, slaughtering whites right and left. Trepidation supplanted their orgy of guilt. Why should they feel so bad about a few blacks being killed by the police when all of their lives were in danger? Trepidation grew to anger. Were they asking too much to feel safe in their own country, their own homes, living their own lives? Hadn't they done enough for the blacks who were imposed on them by their ancestors? Did they bring the blacks here from Africa? Were they responsible for the actions of their antecedants? Civilization would be a shambles if the sins of the fathers were visited on the children to untold generations. They were fed up with these unwanted blacks and their impossible demands.

Inevitably, this resentment aroused strong, exaggeraged hostilities on both sides of the color line.

CHAPTER 15

An outdoor concert was being presented that warm September Sunday afternoon on the mall at Central Park, and a famous white soprano was singing selections from George Gershwin's "Porgy and Bess" suite. The tremendous standing audience was held spellbound.

⟨ Suddenly, an ignorant-looking black man wearing a soiled t-shirt, patched Levis, and blue canvas sneakers, standing at the northern fringe nearest to Harlem, yelled out: "Why don't you white mothers leave go them slavery-time songs about lazy, sinning black people? You think all we do is dodge work 'n lay up 'n fuck like rabbits all day."⟩ He was a red-eyed brother with a liver-lipped mouth and a long, narrow head, and he had a strong, resonant, carrying voice. He was heard at a considerable distance by people in the audience, and he sounded as though he meant it.

But what he meant, exactly, no one knew, and no one cared to draw him out from the general to the particular. Some white people who had heard him expressed their disapproval by glowering. Several laughed. A tarty-looking young blonde woman giggled, as though she thought that wasn't such a despicable life.

But the black people in his vicinity stared at him incredulously, as though he had taken leave of his senses. One black brother expressed the opinion of them all by saying, "Man, Gershwin wasn't a racist, he was just a thief, man. The music you're hearing is one of our own lullabies."

"Why don't you tend to your own mother-raping business, man, and go on kissing these white mothers' asses if that's what you want."

"I'm just telling you, man."

"Telling me what, man, to kiss these white mother-rapers' asses like you? If I had me a rifle like my real black brother had up on Eighth Avenue that night, I'd stop these white mothers from playing these lo-rating songs."

"Don't lose your black, man," the brother advised.

But there was a young white man nearby who was stung to the quick by this black man's reverence for the insane black murderer of five innocent white cops. He had resented his first outburst, but had kept quiet for fear of making a spectacle of himself. But this public adulation for a black murderer of white men was too much; it sounded too much like Malcolm X's reference to President Kennedy's assassination.

"Where's your gratitude, you black son of a bitch," he shouted angrily. "If it wasn't for us white people, you wouldn't be alive. You black bastards live on our sufferance. We feed you, clothe you, house you, educate you, and take better care of you than any other white majority has taken care of their black minorities in the history of the world."

He was a tall, clean-cut, crew-cut, blonde, blue-eyed young man, obviously from suburbia, and his strong, chiseled features were well-suited for the expression of indignation.

But his suggestion that black people lived on white people's mercy goaded the black man to replying.

"Wouldn't be alive? Why you white murderers would massacre us all if you could find somebody else to clean up your shit."

Any reminder of the recent massacre grated on a tender spot in all the whites' subconsciousness, and the blonde young man was not alone in his fury. He rushed up to the black brother and slapped him sharply across the face. The black people in the vicinity did not understand why the white man had become suddenly enraged because all the black man had done was told the truth, but none of them wanted to become involved in a fracas which they thought would blow over after a few insults were passed.

But the black man retaliated with violence instead of words. He whipped a spring-blade knife from the watch pocket of his jeans and slashed at the white man's throat. The white man jerked his head back in time to save himself from serious injury, but still caught the blade across the tip of his chin. Blood showered over his white shirt and seersucker coat. Women screamed.

A broad-assed cop, paunch hanging down over his cartridge belt, hairy forearms exposed beneath the cut-off sleeves of his blue summer shirt, pushed people aside as he tried to get to the fracas. Black people antagonized him with their hostile stares. Then he saw the slashed white man covered with blood, looking as though his throat were cut, and the black man holding him at bay with his knife slashing through the air. He drew his .38 calibre police revolver that hung from the holster at his hip. Maybe he intended to shoot the black man, maybe not. But another black man thought he intended to do so and knocked the gun out of his hand. The cop swung at him with his left hand and the brother grappled with the cop. They wrestled back and forth for a moment, then fell to the ground. When the cop tried to reach for his revolver, which lay a short distance from his outstretched hand, the black man kicked it out of his reach and they began rolling furiously around on the ground. A black sister saw the revolver lying there and, with a quick, sly motion, picked it up and put it in her purse. What possessed her at that moment, no one ever learned, for she began walking swiftly away. A white woman who had seen her pick up the gun and put it into her purse, ran after her, crying, "She's got the policeman's pistol . . . She picked up the policeman's pistol . . ." Several white people looked at her undecidedly, looked at the disappearing back of the black woman, then shrugged and returned their attention to the struggles that were taking place.

Other white men joined their blood-stained confederate in seeking to contain the black man with the knife, but, since they were all unarmed, the black man lunged forward and slashed gleefully at them. The white men drew back nimbly and dodged artfully. The combined actions of them all evoked the performance of a spirited adagio dance, in which the black man dances the role of an irate woman who tries to mark her fickle, feckless lovers, the white men, with the sign of infidelity. But it was not a harmless dance, and two of the white men who were not sufficiently artful in their dodging were slashed on their faces.

None of the slashed men were seriously injured, but their rich, red American blood flowed so copiously that it seemed as though they were being hacked to death by a black savage.

The white spectators watching the action were appalled. "Police! Police!" they cried, much to the amusement of the black spectators who knew from experience that not much blood was actually being lost.

Two of the dozens of cops policing the tremendous crowd had finally become alerted to the scuffle, and were valiantly trying to push through the crowd to do their duty. It may have been a compliment to the popularity of the white soprano—or perhaps to Gershwin—or the arias of the black opera—that they were completely blocked.

Fortunately, a young, athletically-inclined, working-class white man had sufficient presence of mind to slip up behind the black man and tackle him about the legs. He paid for this *beau geste* with a slashed skull, but at least he brought down the black assailant so that he could be disarmed.

"Keep hold of the knife!" cried a white woman. "Keep

hold of the knife!" She was the same woman who had seen the black sister walk off with the first white cop's revolver, and she spoke with authority. "Keep hold of his knife!"

Not only did the blonde young man with the slashed chin take possession of the knife, but he flaunted it in the black man's face and threatened to cut out his nuts and feed them to the squirrels.

But his four companions were not animal lovers, so they let the black man keep his nuts, no doubt to the frustration of local squirrels, and rolled him over on his face so they could tie his wrists together with a tie and bind his ankles with a belt.

Now that the white spectators were relieved to find the white combatants had not been hacked to death, they watched the proceedings with intense fascination. However, the black spectators remained calm, but they found nothing amusing about the spectacle, because it wasn't funny anymore.

The white worker, staunching the flow of blood from his slashed skull with a spare t-shirt he always carried—perhaps because he always expected the worst—suddenly spied a coil of rope attached to a chair. It was used by the park attendants to secure the park chairs at night, but now it sparked the white worker with a bright idea. "Let's hang the nigger."

The other five men of the group had graduated from the hanging class, or more probably had never belonged to it. Nevertheless, they discerned instantly the potential in the suggestion. Here were the ingredients for a tremendous joke: a coil of rope, a tree overhead, and a trussed nigger.

"Sure thing," agreed the blonde with the slashed chin who had appointed himself spokesman for the others. Winking at the white worker, to insure there were no misunderstandings, he added, "You get the rope."

The white spectators instantly recognized the joke. Smiles spread over their faces as they anticipated a new kind of minstrel show that parodied a lynching.

The black spectators became sullen and angry at this racist comedy, and their faces darkened until they were even black enough to suit themselves.

The white worker came forward with the coil of rope, along with the chair to which it was attached, and tauntingly uncoiled it before the black man's gaze. The black was still securely pinioned by the knees of the other white men in his back, but his eyes were glued to the rope like the eyes of a bird being hypnotized by a snake. Slowly uncoiling the rope, draining the last drop of sadism from the scene, the white worker intoned solemnly, "Got anything to say before we hang you, nigger?"

"Yeah, lemme fuck your mama for the last time," the black man said defiantly.

Smiling, the white worker began fashioning a slip noose in the end not attached to the chair. "This'll make you come, nigger," Then to the others he said, "Put the nigger in the chair."

When the black man was lifted into the chair attached to

the rope, the smiles left the faces of the white spectators and they shivered with a tremor of apprehension. A stir of protest went through the assemblage, quick bodily movements, half-finished gestures, tentative steps, grimaces of revulsion. But suddenly they were immobilized by the sight of the slip noose being lowered over the black man's head and tightened about his neck.

"That's not funny," a white woman cried.

The white worker grinned defiantly and threw the other end of the rope over the limb of the tree above them.

"That's gone far enough," a seedy-looking, middle-aged white man shouted with as much authority as he could muster, and took an indignant step.

Behind the black man's head, the blonde man with the slashed chin and bloodstained clothing made a gesture denying that hanging was their real intention and to cap it off, winked reassuringly. Fearing that he might not be understood, he shaped the words with his lips, distorting his face into grimaces as though he were chewing a hunk of alum. "We—just—want—to—scare—the—shit—out—the—black—sonofabitch."

The white spectators gave no sign that they were reassured; they continued to look anxious and disapproving.

The black spectators were becoming hostile, but it appeared as though they were restrained from violent action by a hypnotic terror that seemed to envelope them, and stun their brains, and incapacitate their muscles. It was the pure and simple thought of lynching that immobilized them, memories that were deeply ingrained in their subconsciousness.

Ironically, the vast majority of the people in the audience were sublimely ignorant of anything at all that may be happening on the upper fringe of the crowd, other than an occasional boisterous outburst from one of the black residents of Harlem.

And thus the incident would have ended, had it not been for four long-haired, black-clad, outlaw bikers. They simply were not satisfied with leaving it as it was.

They had paused in pushing their Harley-Davidson motorcycles across the grass, in complete defiance of posted orders to the contrary, to watch the mock lynching. The thought occurred to all of them at once, "What are these buggers playing at?"

On the left breasts of their black leather jackets were stitched yellow labels with the words "DEATH RIDERS," and on the right breasts Nazi crosses, outlined in luminous paint. Their faces were long and narrow, their eyes deepset and dark with black circles beneath them, and one had a long, scraggling black beard. Each had pimply white skin, deeply ingrained with dirt.

The bearded one, who was evidently the leader, jerked his head in the direction of the trussed black man who had been placed in a chair with a noose around his neck, and said "Let's give black power a boost." The others grinned their agreement.

The bearded one pushed his motorcycle underneath the

tree and looped the dangling end of the hanging rope about its frame beneath the handlebars. Then, as he mounted it, the three others chanted "'Sieg Heil!"

It was a four-cylinder motorcycle with a 750 cc engine and a frame strong enough to hold a pyramid of twenty-four men. When he gunned the motor, it took off with a shower of grass and gravel, pulling the hanging rope at burning velocity, and jerked the body of the black man into the air so rapidly it was still in a sitting position as it shot upward. Evidently, the hangman's knot had twisted the neck, for the head was dangling to one side when it smashed upward into the limb of the tree. The neck broke with a loud, eerie cracking, like a tree exploding from frost. Probably it was intensified by the sound of the skull bursting.

The biker was flung ass-over-teakettle across the handlebars and rolled several yards across the grass as the rope jerked the motorcycle upright like a rearing stallion and the rear wheel ran out from under it. The loop slipped over the handlebars when the motorcycle fell on its side and wheeled about in concentric circles, knocking half a dozen spectators off their feet.

Screams punctured the air and pendemonium gripped everyone, black and white alike. But the Death Riders kept their cool. While the bearded rider was getting to his feet, his three companions wrestled the loco motorcycle to a standstill, cut the engine, and stood it on its wheels. The rider limped back and mounted it. His companions mounted theirs.

"I sailed him," the bearded rider boasted, grinning proudly.

"You rocketed him," a companion testified. Grinning together, they gunned their motorcycles across the grass, left the park, and went across the wide asphalt street of Central Park West, disappearing in the direction of the Hudson River before anyone had noticed what they looked like.

how could anyone miss it?

CHAPTER 16

The press made the customary furor over the lynching. Probably the type was already set up for just such a contingency. Much indignation. Much consolation for the family of the lynched man. Such stirring condolences. Such touching essays on the rights of man. The press asked pointed questions, too. Is our society sick? Would a strong, healthy society permit a citizen to be lynched simply for expressing his opinion? Did this not demonstrate the malaise this nation was suffering? And where were the police? The press insisted that more vigilant policing of large public functions was required in view of the state of the nation. All that sort of bullshit.

But in the black community, the lynching precipitated a veritable deluge of reprisals. Black men began running amok and shooting white people right-left-and-center.

A black student at the University of Mississippi holed up in the administration building and shot and killed three members of the faculty and four white seniors—two male and two female—before finally being shot dead from behind by a state trooper who had managed to sneak through a rear window.

A black Baptist minister in Washington, D. C., endeavored to shoot up a number of congressmen, but being ignorant of the customs of congressmen and a pretty poor shot, he only succeeded in shooting five secret servicemen, four of whom survived, and eleven tourists, seven of whom were women, none of whom were killed. He was finally destroyed by a hand grenade that a white visitor from Texas was carrying in his pocket as a defense against black robbers.

A Black Nationalist shooting from the window of a flat beneath a Chinese restaurant at the corner of Sutter and Filmore in San Francisco fired into a parade of the Benevolent Protective Order of Elks as they marched down the hill of Sutter Street. Soon, dead Elks filled the street below. The fusillade was ended when the black was scalded blind by a pot of boiling oil dumped onto his head by the Chinese chef from above, and subsequently hacked into bits by the rest of the Chinese personnel.

A black father of eleven children in the Brownsville section of Brooklyn shot into a group of white elementary school teachers engaged in a lunch hour confab and killed two and wounded seventeen before being shot dead by the two dozen police assigned to the school to keep order and who, as it happens, had been playing pinochle in an empty classroom when the shooting began.

A black handyman in Susanville, California, shot into a

group of Ku Klux Klansmen burning a cross on the front lawn of the boarding house where he was living, killing nine of them outright while one, seriously wounded, escaped. Then, turning the rifle on himself, he squeezed the trigger with his toe, blowing off the top of his own head.

A black doctor, a general practitioner in the black belt in Chicago, drove his Cadillac Fleetwood down to the Loop and parked it opposite the Detective Bureau, calmly unpacked a loaded automatic rifle, rolled the front window halfway down, balanced the gun barrel on the glass, and calmly shot dead every white detective who emerged from the building until a modern English-made tank imported by the Chicago Police for riot control rattled into the Loop, shot, and completely destroyed the black Fleetwood, its black driver, and the entire office building behind it, killing twenty-nine white office workers and injuring thirty-seven others in the process.

A black HEW administrator in Cleveland locked himself in the reinforced ultra-security cell block for convicted murderers in the Cayahoga County Jail and began systematically shooting down anyone with a white face, with the exception of the prisoners, who came within his sight, including prison guards, county officials, state's attorneys, probation officers, not to mention city police. A tank from the Ohio State National Guard was brought in but it could not be maneuvered into effective range and was only destroying sections of the country courthouse with its 105 mm cannon, before it was called off. In the end, officials resorted to bombing, and a B-52 bomber was sent from Wright-Patterson Airfield, and the Cayahoga County Jail was blown out of existence.

It was inevitable that the forces of law and order would over-react to the killers. And as the black maniacs went on shooting sprees in more and more sections of the white community, the uncontrollable tendency by the forces of law and order to over-kill was responsible for five times as many deaths of innocent white people then those killed by the black maniacs themselves. In the end, it became evident to all that the forces of law and order would eventually decimate their own race if not restrained.

But what the white community found more staggering was the discovery that not only did these black maniacs have no particular segment of the white community they wished to destroy, but that they, themselves, were not of the same type and class. There was no common denominator. They were blacks from all classes, from all levels of education, from all walks of life, from all economic levels—the poor, the ugly, the rich and the handsome. And they not only hated the white police, as the white community had long since assumed, they hated whites of all ages and sexes. They hated the white economy, the white culture, the white religion, and white civilization in general. This realization shocked and frightened the white community more than anything.

What was more, these black killers were inconsistent in the selection of their victims. What had congressmen to do with a black minister? What had a Black Nationalist got against white Elks? This wasn't the jungle. He didn't want to eat them. And what had a successful black doctor got against the Chicago Police? He wasn't a civil rights worker. He had never been arrested. He had never even been third-degreed. It was all very confusing.

CHAPTER 17

The questions that presented themselves to the forces of law and order were who, why, and how.

In most instances, despite the fact that the black killers were mutilated beyond recognition, they had left sufficient clues to be identified. The question of who they were presented no problem. (The police knew immediately who they were, and this information was speedily transmitted to the public: they were black bastards who had gone insane, that's who.)

But the question who? precipitated the question why? Why had these black citizens—an alarming number of whom had been educated, intelligent, affluent, and successful in all the ways success is computed in the American way of life—embarked upon this suicidal, insane course of killing innocent, unengaged, unknown white strangers? If whites had injured them, insulted them, abused them, persecuted them, or offended them in any manner or form, it would have made some kind of sense. But the whites these blacks had killed had been total strangers; they had not had an opportunity to incur any black hatred. They had been bystanders, they had been killed without purpose or point, they had been killed without being known, they had been killed like so many birds flying by a cretin who just liked to hear the sound of his gun.

This information, dutifully transmitted to the public, inspired much soul searching in the white community. What had whites done to incur such murderous hatred by blacks? They had never heard the plaintive song sung by Louis Armstrong: "What did I do to be so black and blue?" What had they done to be so hated by blacks? There might have been misunderstandings between the races, but not of sufficient virulence to bring on these insane outbursts.

What if they had segregated the blacks? Was that a capital offense? Didn't the blacks want to be to themselves? Weren't many of the blacks even now petitioning for autonomy? Wasn't segregation the same as autonomy? And even to themselves they denied having ever persecuted the blacks or oppressed them. They had been permitted to grow up as blacks, live as blacks, die as blacks. Was that oppression? Could they have lived and died as whites even if they had been permitted? Was it possible? Were not the blacks of this nation better off than blacks in any other nation in the world with a white majority? In fact, were their lives not richer, more purposeful, and happier than even the lives of blacks in Africa with their own governments and societies? A serious study of the comparison of the lives of American blacks to the lives of whites in a majority of the nations in the civilized world might well reveal that American blacks were better off than the majority of all the whites in the rest of the world. Was that oppression?

Why then, had these blacks embarked on such a senseless course of killing whites when it would only lead to death for themselves and untold hardships for their race? What could they possibly hope to gain?

An objective sociologist might have noted that the first case of these unrestrained outbursts of killing by black men had been by an unnamed, unknown, seemingly ignorant black man who had appeared to be completely unemotional about killing and totally indifferent about being killed. That might have told the white community something.

The forces of law and order were not as preoccupied with the question of "why?" as was the white community as a whole. "Why?" was the question for the courts of law, the various state and federal legislators. The question which presented itself to the forces of law and order was how? How had these killings taken place? How had these blacks arrived at the actual sites of their outbursts? Had they walked, carrying the guns in their arms? Had they rode? Had they flown? Had they had help? And how had they come in possession of these dangerous guns? That was the question. All the others were incidental.

All the guns were of the same make, unmarked army field rifles similar to the U. S. M-14, shooting a 7.62 calibre cartridge. None carried any clues. Nor were any clues relating to the guns discovered in the residences of the dead black killers. Neither families, wives, children, friends, acquaintences, servants, or neighbors admitted to any previous knowledge of any kind concerning the guns. No one admitted ever having seen them before; no one admitted having seen the delivery of the florist's boxes in which they had come; no one admitted having noticed anything unusual in the behavior, the demeanor, or the habits of the black killers before they had gone on their rampages and been killed. No one admitted any to knowledge or act that may have connected them in any way to the shootings. No one admitted having seen anything, heard anything, known anything, or done anything which could be construed as incriminating.

Law enforcement agencies were baffled but not surprised. Under the circumstances, they hadn't expected anyone would voluntarily testify to any knowledge or behavior which might very well get himself in the soup. As a consequence, they proceeded with their own private investigations.

The assistance of the FBI was requested by a joint petition of all the police departments in cities where the shootings had taken place.

In due course, the FBI interrogated all registered manufacturers of guns and ammunition within the territorial boundaries of the U. S., and diligently searched for clandestine manufacturers, but none were discovered. The manufacturer and sale of arms and ammunition were sufficiently profitable in the U. S. to discourage its being done illegitimately. But not one firm admitted any knowledge of that particular gun, although the type was familiar enough.

No thefts of such guns had been reported, which was was no surprise, since no retailer admitted selling or ever having seen such guns. There was no evidence of their having been smuggled into the U. S., or even any hints that pointed in that direction.

The CIA undertook to discover where such guns and ammunition may have been produced in other nations, and it did not take long to establish that no such manufacturers existed anywhere in the western world. Of course, the guns might have originated from behind the Iron Curtain or inside Red China, but its spy network was unable to uncover any information in this respect whatsoever.

The CIA passed the ball back to the FBI, which was responsible for internal security. The FBI decided that if they could not discover the original source of the guns, they might at least uncover the means by which they were distributed. It appeared obvious that the distribution was carried out by some agency, for no individual could possibly have the means or organization to undertake such an operation.

But there were many organizations capable of such an undertaking, both politically and physically. Of course, it required a certain type of mentality that was strictly the opposite of the common, patriotic, conformist mentality of the average American. From both a physical and political standpoint, it seemed likely that the organization behind the killings had to be an agency with communist or anti-white orientation, but it was also possible that it might be some misguided group of the extreme right who hated blacks and desired to set them up for extermination.

The first agencies the FBI staked out were the John Birch Society, the Ku Klux Klan, the Communist Party, the Friends of Cuba and North Vietnam Committees, and the American Nazi Party. But they were shortly to establish what they had already suspected: that all these agencies had the same kind of harmless, domesticated natures that an old horse has; primarily gentle and loyal but with an occasional desire to kick out and pretend he is a vicious stallion. None wanted to see the demise of the establishment.

However, the major part of its investigation centered on Black Nationalistic groups and black militant groups which had acquired a political standing. Among these were the Black Foxes, the Black Torchbearers, the Black Avengers, the Black Arts-Culture-History (BACH), the Black World, and a small group of black fanatics that called themselves the Black Death.

Impressive caches of arms and ammunition, explosives, and drugs of a kind known as "Truth Serums," used for interrogations, were uncovered in the headquarters of most of these groups. Sidearms—pistols and revolvers—hunting guns, a few artillery pieces such as mortars, bazookas, .50 calibre water-cooled machine guns, and enough plastic explosive to blow up the Mississippi River were discovered, but no automatic rifles of the type sought. This surprised the FBI, in view of the fact that there was such an abundance of other weapons.

But the FBI did not reveal its discoveries to the public for fear of disturbing it further, choosing to simply call in armed forces to quietly clean out the arms caches and arrest all blacks in the vicinity. When it finally became convinced that no known black group of political militancy was responsible for the distrubution of the "murder weapons," as the automatic rifles had come to be known, there was only one other well-known American agency left. And it was the toughest kind to investigate, because it was invisible. It was the "Conspiracy."

But search as it would, no conspiracy was uncovered. And the source of the guns remained a mystery.

CHAPTER 18

The white community was not only disturbed but it was confused. The forces of law and order sworn to protect them from the blacks were, in fact, killing more of them through excesses of over-kill and over-reaction. The deaths of these innocent victims, those killed by the insane blacks and those killed by the over-zealous white police, threw the white community into the same slough of grief and despair as it had suffered at the time of the black massacre. But now, added to their guilt was fear, not only of the blacks and the consequences of containing them, but of themselves, the excesses that they, the normal white majority, might be pushed into committing. And over and above all, apart even from their instinctive racial reactions of guilt, fear, and re-vulsion, was the emotion inspired by the mystery of the guns. It was an emotion of extreme uneasiness stemming from the suspicion that something might be happening in the world that they didn't know about—happening to them. Where were the guns coming from? Who was arming these irresponsible blacks? And for what purpose? Were they, the American white community, targets of some diabolical communist scheme for weakening the U. S. militarily? Were blacks being used for the destruction of capitalism? Was the attack aimed at Authority, Democracy, or all the pillars of American Society? Were they the victims of a conspiracy by all the blacks who inhabited the earth? The white community knew and feared conspiracies, although most white people had never seen one. Or was Red China the nigger in the woodpile?

But regardless of where the guns were coming from, the first act of self-preservation was to discover who had them. The blacks must be searched one by one for possession. A strategy similar to that of the "search and destroy" in Vietnam must be undertaken in the U. S. The black bastards who had guns in their possession must be found and destroyed.

There was an immediate demand for larger police forces. More sophisticated weapons which would not subject the white community to needless danger were needed. Domestic security should take precedence over national security. The white community petitioned Congress to suspend the manufacture and stockpiling of nuclear weapons, continental ballistic missiles, and Polaris submarines, and concentrate on developing atomic bombs that could be used to destroy one black bastard with a gun without subjecting the entire white community to danger. An atom bomb that could be carried in a policeman's pocket with his blackjack and which would not produce any radioactivity when it exploded.

In the meantime, conventional weapons and exercises could be employed to scour the black ghettoes for dangerous weapons and at the same time screen individual blacks for dangerous attitudes. Small armed tanks with the latest in anti-riot devices, such as anti-riot glue to immobilize rioters by sticking them together in balls of ten or twelve each, paralyzing gas, sneezing powders to incapacitate rioters with paroxysms of sneezing, sprays to temporarily blind anyone who resisted an order, and electronic devices similar to Geiger counters which reacted only to the combined pulsations from black skin and blue steel, for use in the location of black killers with guns, were all needed by police to patrol the streets. House-to-house searches were made of all black residences, no matter how humble, and no black was safe with a piece of iron larger than a nail cutter, unless he was adroit enough to win the time to talk. And still the white community demanded that local police forces be supported by the national armed forces. At the same time, they deplored any excess which might deprive blacks of their civil rights.

In due time, all blacks were required to register with the police and were meticulously screened for anti-white attitudes. And woe betide the black who was discovered to resist eating rice or drinking milk because it was white. Blacks found guilty of anti-white attitudes were summarily locked in stockades that had been constructed for that purpose. Those who were listed as doubtful were issued yellow cards that permitted them freedom of the street at certain hours of the day, but at night restricted them to their houses. Only those that the other blacks castigated as "Uncle Toms" were classified by the police as dependable and given green cards that permitted them as much freedom as they had known before. However, they were required to spy, not only on doubtful blacks, but on one another. From this arose so much suspicion that, superficially at least, the black race appeared to be both deaf and dumb.

And yet the white community continued to suffer such fear, guilt, and insecurity, that the very stability of their society was threatened. Many whites became ill and haggard from emotional insecurity. Others retained their sanity through the therapeutic remedy of nightmares, for during this terrible period, whites experienced a variety of assorted nightmares, all of which featured the enlarged sexual organs of black males.

One white woman dreamed that a black had gouged out one of her breasts and was thrusting his enormous black penis, which had two thick, brutal horns, into the bloody hole.

A middle-aged white advertising executive dreamed that a giant nude black, with testicles hanging from his crotch like huge black bombs, was coming toward him, firing from a disembodied penis as big as a cannon barrel. He could feel each of the big solid bullets as it penetrated his body.

Another white woman, a young matron with two lovely children, dreamed that when she had gone out onto the street, she was engulfed by a squirming mass of black pythons. When she screamed for her husband to save her, he appeared soaring overhead, exploding like a brilliant burst of fireworks. In despair, she quit struggling against the pythons and resigned herself to her fate. When she looked at them again, however, she suddenly recognized them as squirming black penises.

In this atmosphere of intense guilt and fear, blacks became deathly afraid of the whites' fear. The black man had always feared the white man's fear. Added to it, now, were guilt and insecurity, which rendered it even more dangerous and unpredictable. ~~Roosevelt mocked Lenin~~

Blacks became afraid to pass whites on the sidewalk. Invariably they stepped off into the street. When a tank came down a ghetto street, blacks scurried for cover like rats. Possession of a green card did not quiet their fear of white fear. There was an instinctive quality about this fear, as though it were hereditary and had come down through centuries from generation to generation. Black children acted as though they had been born with it. Blacks who could neither read nor write and knew nothing of the history of the white man were possessed with it. Those blacks who had learned of the exploitation of blacks by whites throughout the centuries had also learned that when they suffered from fear and guilt, whites were as dangerous and undiscriminating as blind rattlesnakes. Black people went underground, the good, the bad, and the ugly.

However, at first there had been a few Uncle Toms who, thinking themselves in the good graces of the whites and wishing to remain so, reported the receipt of guns. They rushed with their guns to the nearest police station and told how the guns had been thrust into their hands by black messengers who had then disappeared. They expected an accolade, a pat on the head, or at least a commendation for being good niggers, but when it was discovered that they could not tell the whites the source of the guns—which none of them knew—the whites turned on them with insensate fury and beat them damn near to death. They were subjected to extensive third degrees and brutal torture. Some had their tongues cut out because they wouldn't tell what they didn't know. Others had their eyes gouged out because they couldn't report what they hadn't seen. Others had their hands chopped off, some were castrated, some were beaten so brutally they never regained their senses. They were stripped of their property, separated from their families, their green cards were confiscated, they were denied work, and deprived of shelter. They scarcely survived on the crumbs they could beg from the uncooperative, sullen blacks who had kept their mouths shut. Thereafter, even the rankest, most obsequious Uncle Tom knew better than to report receiving one of the dangerous guns to the white police.

It was even more dangerous to be caught in possession of one of the offensive weapons. It was worse than being caught with the bubonic plague, or more lethal anyway. The guns were more dangerous as malignant objects then they were as offensive weapons. They were, in some ways, similar to sixteen pounds of radium. Just being near one was dangerous, and the wages of owning one was instantaneous death.

Frantically, blacks began ridding themselves of these deadly objects. They shied and shuddered at the sight of one. They fled from their vicinity, but they soon discovered it was not as easy to get rid of them as it was to get hold of one. The guns had been placed in their possession with ease and subtlety, but getting rid of them was just the opposite.

They were too bulky to hide, too solid to melt. They were too heavy to be painted and camouflaged as a child's toy. In most instances, there was neither an ocean, a lake, a river, or even a well in which they could be quietly dropped. They were forced to leave them in the streets, in tenement hallways, doorways, basements, and rooftops. They threw them down drains, into manholes, garbage cans, parked cars, and through open windows into other blacks' flats. They broke into other flats to hide them under beds, in closets, behind furnishings, anywhere to get rid of them. It became every man for himself. Some ghettoes became so thick with abandoned guns, that the forces of law and order might have given up hope of ever containing the black population, had the guns remained hidden.

In consequence, blacks became afraid to walk down a deserted street because of the risk of being caught near an abandoned gun. They became afraid to return home for fear of finding another gun abandoned there. Meticulously they searched every room and closet and piece of furniture of any flat they entered. They searched the interiors of cars that had been parked and peered beneath the chassis before driving off. Whenever they found a gun concealed in their dwellings or on their properties, they would quickly dump it somewhere else.

They lived in an atmosphere of fear of the whites and suspicion of each other that had, itself, been caused by white fear. It was like a deadly carousel.

Paradoxically, it was the whites' guilt and fear that eventually saved blacks from extermination. The whites had the means, but they did not have the will. Their guilt would not permit them to exterminate the black race. They were more afraid of their own moral condemnation than they were of the danger blacks posed to them. They would have granted all black demands, but they were afraid of the violent objections of other whites. They had no positive proof that these violent objections existed, but they believed in them like they believed in conspiracies. It was in this belief they persisted.

The white majorities of the other nations of the world, particularly those European nations considered most closely aligned to America's white majority, were appalled by what they considered an irrational approach to an uprising by a black minority. While Americans suffer guilt over black segregation and restriction, in other white societies the assumption of black equality is summarily dismissed. This is why other white majorities treat their black minorities with greater consideration and politeness. They do not fear that blacks will ever attain equality or that they will even request it.

Strangely enough, American blacks don't know this, and probably most whites don't, either.

It was perhaps inevitable that blacks would eventually turn on the mysterious messengers who brought them so much danger and hardship. However, the appearance of the messengers had changed since that fateful rifle had been delivered to T-bone Smith. Now they were not as easy to identify, or even remember, as they had been. As relations between whites and blacks had grown increasingly tense, the appearance of the messengers had gradually metamorphized from the neatly uniformed, purposeful black youths. First, they appeared as older, slovenly, disinterested men, then gradually to younger men of greater physical agility but little intellectual acuity. All were dressed in the uniform of the unemployed relief recipient—patched blue jeans, soiled blue T-shirt, scuffed blue canvas sneakers—in other words, the type who could instantly disappear into a crowd. Had they given it any thought, blacks would have quickly concluded that this had been done to give the messengers greater protection. However, most blacks thought only that they were misled numbskulls bent on getting them all into trouble, and as such, that they could be stopped.

But how? This new crop of messengers proved to be quick, strong, and single-minded. They came out of no-where, always after dark, when the streets were empty of blacks and when white patrols were slack. They thrust the dreaded guns into their recipients' hands and melted back into the darkness from whence they had come. Woe betide any recipient who should try to stop them. Most times the messenger would simply disable the recipient with a few lightening quick karate chops and leave him floundering on the floor.

When the recipient was a quick, strong, athletic man, equal to the messenger's physical prowess, the messenger would simply draw a .22 calibre revolver and shoot him dead. Soon it became apparent that there was greater danger in trying to capture the messenger than in receiving the gun. In that case, at least, the recipient had time and dark-ness in which to dispose of the gun.

Nevertheless, some wildly dramatic scenes ensued as some blacks persisted in trying to capture a messenger. Men dressed in jeans and T-shirts, seemingly like any other out-of-work black man, were often seen fleeing from mobs of other black men, invariably led by a man bleeding profusely from a variety of wounds until he collapsed. In rare in-stances, black messengers were captured by their pursuers, and some were summarily lynched by the friends of the men they had killed. However, this was nothing compared to the pain inflicted by the police when one of these messengers was turned over to them.

In these instances, the police were not restrained by public opinion. Messengers were sometimes flayed, layer by layer, until the white bone showed through. Some lost their eyes, one by one, their finger and toe nails, one by one, their teeth, one by one, their sexual organs, their hands and feet. Some of these victims of insensate white rage even lost their heads. It was rumored that the severed heads of black men had been seen on display in front of precinct stations, sometimes accompanied by a severed pair of hands, black testicles hanging from a string, severed black feet paired sedately on a cardboard carton beside the precinct steps.

These were seen only by blacks in the ghettoes. Even had they heard of any such rumors, no white man would have believed them, since suicidal black killers continued to surface. The more the killings continued, the more the white community panicked, and the more ludicrous became their demands. Eventually whites demanded that many large, modern prisons be erected all over the United States, and that all blacks be locked up in them, except for the few needed to look after their food and sanitation. These few had to be carefully screened and only those blacks who could pass a series of stringent tests that proved they were reliable Uncle Toms would be accepted. However, the government rejected this demand on the grounds that too many whites would be deprived of their servants.

CHAPTER 19

As soon as Tomsson Black cashed Barbara's check, he moved uptown to Harlem and rented the entire first floor of a new office building on 125th Street. While the seven offices were being furnished with the latest in office equipment, he had all of the doors opening onto the corridor, along with the windows fronting on 125th Street inscribed with the legend:

BLACK FOR BLACKS, INC.

T. Black, President

Afterward, he staffed the offices with young black men and women, all under the age of thirty. As soon as he was established, the blacks of Harlem flocked in to express their support. Not because of the nature of his business, for none of them knew exactly what it was, but simply because he was a big, impressive-looking man, a man of distinction with an undeniable air of confidence. Because he was gregarious and courteous and at home among blacks and approachable by all. Because he had been convicted and sentenced to life for raping a white woman but hadn't let it destroy him. Because after only three years imprisonment he was back among his own people, rich and purposeful and obviously powerful.

Many of them admired him because they still remembered his revolutionary background and that his doctrine had always been death to the whiteys. But mostly they came to see him because he was black, black as a man can be, black as any of them, and even his name was "Black."

There was no one on Tomsson Black's office staff except personable young black people. He knew he was being unfair to the light-skinned and mulatto black people, but he wanted to be surrounded by young people who were as black as himself. It was part of his plan. In time he might work up to employing light-skinned black people. In fact, if his plans matured it would be unavoidable. But he wanted to start with the blackest of the black. The young people in his office might have been the winners of a black beauty contest.

They felt a special respect for him, and they loved and admired him, too. They thought him so handsome and self-assured that they were eager to please him. To him, that was the most important thing.

All of them had been to college. Some had attended all-black schools in the South, others had attended colleges and universities in the North. There were several young men who had attended Columbia University, and several young women who had attended Hunter College, and several of both sexes who had attended City College. But he showed no favoritism.

In the beginning he put them to work researching all of the recorded research on the meat-packing industry in the United States; its inception and its development, its operation and management, its products and by-products, its waste and its profits. These young blacks loved him and admired him and respected him, but they thought he had gone nuts.

When he gave them their next assignment they were sure of it. This was the researching of all the known processes of land reclamation, the researching and copying of all Alabama State laws governing the ownership of land, title deeds and taxes, Federal laws defining territorial waters that listed the uses and control of such waters as regards fishing and mineral rights, and the regulations applying to navigation.

After studying their findings, he assigned them to draw up a prospectus for the construction and operation of a pig farm and packing house that would employ all modern techniques for breeding and raising pigs, processing and packaging pork products and by-products, and distributing such products to all sections of the United States. They were to include the constuction of the buildings, the type and cost of the equipment needed, and the nature of the transport required. The prospectus was to be based on the assumption that one hundred thousand people would be employed in its operation. By then they began to wonder what he had in mind, but no one dared ask.

When they had drawn up the prospectus and mimeographed five hundred copies, he mailed a copy to each of the black leaders in the United States, regardless of their political affiliation, political belief, opinions on the right course for black progress, opinions on each other and on the whites. To each he explained that this project would be non-profit making, and that its sole purpose would be that of employing indigent blacks and taking them off the relief rolls and other forms of white charity.

Without waiting for their replies, he went to Mobile, Alabama, and consulted the county registry of title deeds to ascertain the owner of the old Harrison place. As he had expected, the place was intestate and for many years had been offered for sale at fifty cents an acre to pay the back taxes. He paid twenty-five hundred dollars in cash and had the title deed made out to George Washington Lincoln, his former name.

A crowd of redneck clerks from all the other offices in the courthouse, who were familiar with the place and its reputation, gathered to look at the "half-witted northern nigger" who had twenty-five hundred dollars to throw away. He didn't even give them the satisfaction of hearing his "Yankee" speech. He silently pocketed his title deed and walked to the railway station where he entrained to the north and back to Harlem. He had not even taken the time to look at the Harrison place, which he had never seen.

Answers awaited him from most of the black leaders to whom he had sent copies of his prospectus. All expressed enthusiasm about the project that would employ a hundred thousand indigent blacks, but most contained suspicions concerning his motives and intentions. He did not reply to any of them.

His next step was to contact a firm of white engineers in downtown Manhattan and employ a team of ten surveyors and two engineers whom he sent to Mobile with instructions to survey the old Harrison place and mark the boundaries. The two engineers were instructed to make an appraisal of the feasibility and cost of clearing and reclaiming the land, building a pier along the boundary bordering on Mobile Bay, and concrete roads leading from it to the boundary opposite.

They went on their assignment equipped with jungle paraphenalia, including boots and suits resistant to snakebite and other poisons, weapons to protect them from the sharp-toothed razorback and boar hogs, pumas, bears, and other wild beasts, anti-toxins and lotions and mosquito net masks and every other protection and medication they deemed necessary for a jungle expedition. The only contingency they had not anticipated were the inquisitive local rednecks who came out *en masse* to stare at them and get in their way as they proceeded about their work.

The surveyors marked the boundaries with concrete posts one hundred yards apart and the engineers estimated it would cost in the neighborhood of five hundred thousand dollars to reclaim the land and to build a pier and the roads that Tomsson Black had proposed. Like all the others in the engineering firm, they thought Tomsson Black represented an organization of blacks who wished to build a housing development for black segregationists.

But he was soon to disillusion them. When they returned from their mission, Tomsson Black presented the firm with his prospectus and asked for an estimate of the total cost of building a pig farm and packing house with facilities for transport, in addition to clearing the land and building the roads. Needless to say, the old white men at the head of the firm were shocked by the nature and the scope of his plan. Nevertheless, they gave him an honest estimate that a minimum of one million dollars would be needed to produce the first cured ham for market.

Incorporating that estimate in the prospectus, Tomsson Black gave his project the name of "CHITTERLINGS, INC." and sent it to the Hull Foundation along with an exposition of its purpose to employ indigent blacks, to apply for a one million dollar grant.

CHAPTER 20

The Hull Foundation had ten billion dollars at its disposal and was the world's richest foundation. Its director, Henry H. Hopkins, former dean of the Harvard University College of Law, was a tall, spare New Englander, whose ancestors had been active in the "Underground Railroad." He had introduced such liberal policies in the operation of the Hull Foundation as to incur the fear and suspicion of many of the nation's leading conservatives. Several right-wing newspaper columnists had gone so far as to call him pink, but he was a fervent apostle of the American way of life and of all its institutions, and he firmly believed the solution to America's "black problem" lay in the capabilities of blacks, themselves, once they discovered them. He believed that by nature of their inheritance and background, blacks had developed a stronger character than whites, but they had not discovered how to exploit it. His greatest hope was that, during his term as director of the Hull Foundation, he would discover a way to endow blacks with the means to fulfill their destiny. He knew that what they needed most in a capitalistic society was capital, and if it ever became possible he would put the full volume of the capital of the Hull Foundation in their hands and let the conservatives castigate him all they would.

When the prospectus for Chitterlings, Inc. and the application for the grant of a million dollars by Tomsson Black reached his desk, he was alarmed. Because of the urgency of the national problem of what to do with indigent blacks, the application deserved consideration. Tomsson Black's plan for creating a profitless meat-packing industry which would employ more than a hundred thousand of them exhibited imagination and understanding, and the prospectus showed that it was feasible. The million dollars would be a comparatively minor endowment, and in view of the anticipated benefits, the application could not be ignored.

But his reaction to the man, Tomsson Black, himself, was strikingly similar to the reaction of the nation's black leaders. From his point of view, the man's motives and intentions were automatically suspect. In many of the nation's leading establishments, the press, charitable and law enforcement institutions, commerce and industry, there was a secret list of the names of all blacks in the news who were classified as "suspects," and Tomsson Black's name headed the list. The name of Tomsson Black was notorious in the United States. He had been a member of every white-hating black group. He had been given tremendous publicity for his vicious and unfounded attacks on the police. He had defied the State Department and visited all the communist countries declared out of bounds to U. S. citizens. And finally, he had savagely raped the wife of a white man who had sought to befriend him and had been sentenced to life in the penetentiary. And now he was out, after what seemed like a disgracefully short time, and had the audacity to apply to the Hull Foundation for a grant of a million dollars.

However, Hopkins refused to let his personal prejudice against the man deter him from giving full consideration to a project that had such great potential for the relief of human misery. He would not pretend that he liked the man. He would treat him courteously but sternly. He would force him to reveal his true motives and intentions. And, if during the process, Tomsson Black became displeased and withdrew his application, the project, in itself, was of such great value that the Hull Foundation would not let it go to waste. They would find another black to foster it, someone whom they could support in all good conscience. Unbeknown to Hopkins, Tomsson Black had already forseen this attitude on his part and had bought the land with his own money and held it in his own name.

First Hopkins contacted the FBI to ask how Tomsson Black had gotten out of prison before the expiration of his sentence. When he was informed that Edward Goodfeller had interceded on his behalf and influenced the governor to grant him a pardon, Hopkins asked the FBI to find out what "hold" Tomsson Black had on Goodfeller, and what other crimes he had been involved in. The FBI was forced to give Tomsson Black a clean bill of health. Goodfeller had interceded for him solely because his conscience troubled him and he and Mrs. Goodfeller had decided that Tomsson Black had paid his debt to society. In point of fact, there were no records of Tomsson Black having ever been involved in any other crime.

Next Hopkins asked the State Department if it had placed any restrictions on Tomsson Black. The State Department replied that he was just listed as "suspect," as he was with all other federal agencies. The department representative humorously noted that it would not nominate him as an ambassador to South Africa.

Hopkins then had all the black leaders listed as "responsible" canvassed for their opinions as to the reliability of Tomsson Black as a person, and the sociological value of his project. All the "responsible" black leaders agreed that as a black individual, Tomsson Black was a disgrace to the black race, but his project had great potential for the improvement of black conditions.

Finally, Hopkins had all the better-known white civic leaders and leading liberal thinkers of industry and commerce canvassed for their opinions as to the value of the project politically and as a service to humanity. The replies from this group were varied. Most agreed that such a project, in reliable hands, would undoubtedly effect a strong rebuttal to communist propaganda against capitalism. Some admitted their inability to assess its value as a service to humanity, but agreed that without a doubt, it would help feed the nation's indigent black population and put them to work. This last opinion afforded Hopkins a sardonic smile. However, the common denominator of all the opinions received was that everyone shared his negative view of Tomsson Black.

Now the time had come to meet Tomsson Black face to face. This meeting between two men so dissimilar in character did not shake the world, but it represented a confrontation between the races in microcosm. The tall, elderly, distinguished-looking white man sat across his wide, polished desk from the much younger, but equally distinguished-looking black man. There the similarity ended. Tomsson Black was dressed in a somber pin-striped black suit of excellent cut, white shirt, black tie, shoes, and socks. Mr. Hopkins wore a wrinkled gray herringbone suit, blue shirt, red tie, and brown shoes. As in most instances, the black man was the more elegant of the two.

But the white man was more at ease. Tomsson Black was cognizant of this fact and he silently cursed himself. Hopkins was also cognizant of it, and endeavored to make him more comfortable. Not because he had any sympathy for the man, but because it seemed he had an unfair advantage accorded by tradition. But as a counterbalance against this unfair advantage, Hopkins felt a reluctant sympathy for this black man who had committed a crime that he could understand. Was there ever a virile black man immune to raping a lush, tantalizing white woman who made herself available?

However, Tomsson Black had armed himself with a shield of defensive dignity. He returned Hopkins' direct, penetrating gaze with one that was equally direct and candid.

Hopkins asked him to elaborate on the benefits that he hoped would be derived from his project and how they could be best achieved.

Tomsson Black contended that his project would prove beneficial to all of society by employing and housing the nation's indigent blacks. On the five thousand acres where the multi-tiered pig farm and packing houses were to be located, a large, modern housing development would be built to accomodate all of the workers and their families. This housing development would be a complex of twenty-storied apartment houses built around a park and public swimming pool, and would include boutiques, apartment stores, supermarkets, all types of service shops from dry cleaners to florists, a bank, a post office, library, hospital, cinemas, and an elementary school with a stadium for sports. The workers would pay a nominal rent, based on the income of the firm, and could partake of all the services and entertainments free of charge. Attendance in the elementary school would be compulsory until the age of sixteen or graduation.

Indigent black people would be recruited from all the black ghettos in the nation; relief rolls and the lists of blacks on private charities would be canvassed and even the needy would be taken from the streets. These people, the father or the mother, the husband or the wife, or both, and single men, single women, and unmarried mothers would be given jobs with the firm and their transportation and that of their children and dependants would be paid to the home plant in Mobile, or to wherever they were to be employed, free of charge. Furnished housing would be waiting on their arrival.

He hoped, in time, to incorporate concurrent programs for the assistance and cure of drug addicts and the rehabilitation of ex-convicts, along with the medical facilities and homes for the infirm and aged who had no assistance.

It was his intention to eventually provide all of the nation's indigent blacks, along with those who became indigent in the future, the opportunity for gainful employment and agreeable, rewarding lives, so that their children, if not themselves, could participate in the full, creative, and exciting life offered by the United States.

Mr. Hopkins was moved by this exposition.

"The commercial accomplishments of Chitterlings, Inc., although necessary for maintenance, are negligible in comparison to the human contribution we wish to make," Tomsson Black concluded.

Hopkins knew that Tomsson Black was a risky character and he suspected that deep down he was disloyal to America and anti-white, besides. He could feel vibrations of evil emanating from his person, but he felt himself being persuaded in spite of it. Tomsson Black might have been a snake, and he, Hopkins, a bird. He wondered if this was the way a woman felt when she was being seduced against her will.

Suddenly he asked, "Do you still bear ill will against Mr. and Mrs. Goodfeller?"

"I never bore them any ill will, sir," Tomsson Black replied without any hint in manner or voice that the question had disturbed him. He spoke as though discussing an exercise in sociology. "I have always considered Mr. and Mrs. Goodfeller as friends and protectors, even during and after the unfortunate business of rape."

Hopkins leaned forward with sudden interest and his color heightened. "Mrs. Goodfeller is a beautiful woman, I understand," he ventured.

"Very beautiful, indeed," Tomsson Black answered with emotion.

"Tell me, did you get any pleasure out of raping her? I mean sexual pleasure." Mr. Hopkins was not normally ashamed of his curiosity, but sometimes, as now, it disturbed him.

"No sir, I became blindly angry at the sight of her body and I thought, 'Is this what so many blacks have been lynched for?' It was just the same as a black woman's body, only the skin was white."

Hopkins caught himself about to rub his hands together with glee. "Was this the first white woman you ever raped?"

"Sir, I do not go about raping white women promiscuously, otherwise I would undoubtedly be dead."

Mr. Hopkins chuckled. "You appear to be a strong, vigorous man."

"I mean shot dead," Tomsson Black corrected him.

Suddenly Mr. Hopkins returned to his previous character of objective, clinical appraisal. "Why did you rape her, then? You said that she and her husband were your friends and protectors."

"She was there," Tomsson Black said in a flat, unemotional voice. Then realizing that Hopkins expected a more logical answer, he elaborated, "She kept walking around her cabin in the nude when she knew I had to pass by. My cabin adjoined theirs."

"Teasing you."

"Well, I don't know whether she was teasing or not, or whether she was inviting me. It is said that black men inspire the baser emotions in white women because they don't consider us as human. Therefore, they can indulge in any depravity at all with us because they believe it doesn't count." His voice had roughened and it was obvious the memory angered him.

"Was she depraved?"

"No sir, but I got angry and began beating her."

"Before you raped her? Or while you were raping her?" Hopkins was shocked to realize that he was deriving a vicarious excitement from this dialogue and he wanted to stop it, but the desire to continue was stronger than his will to stop.

"I don't remember. I just remember she was badly beaten up when her husband came."

"And yet they interceded to have you released from prison."

"Yes sir, but I don't find that surprising. I have learned that white people are the only true Christians on earth. And it is a Christian tenet to forgive."

"And have you forgiven them?"

"Forgiven them for what? It was I who wronged them."

"But they put the flesh pots in your path that tempted you. They plucked you from your native environment and plunged you into a different life, more sophisticated, more permissive, more amoral in a refined fashion."

"I didn't notice all of that. I must be very naive, a primitive at heart. I thought Mr. and Mrs. Goodfeller were just friendly, enlightened people, but very moral and high-principled."

"Just so. I was endeavoring to put myself in your place to understand your attitude toward white people. Tell me, deep in your heart, do you hate us for the way we have exploited you?"

"You mean, do I hate white people?"

"Yes, just that."

"No sir, I think at this point in the history of America, the races are even in their debt to one another. You took us from Africa as slaves, but some of us were already slaves in Africa and would have remained slaves until slavery there was abolished.

"It is true, you brought us here as slaves and worked us as slaves and profited by our sweat," he continued, "but we learned things from you we would never have learned in Africa. We learned trade, we learned Christianity, we learned English, we learned to grow food and build shelter, and eventually we were freed. Now we have acquired more of the blessings of civilization than any other black people of comparable numbers on earth. We American blacks are better fed, better clothed, better housed, better educated, and are more devout Christians than any other blacks on earth.

"We earn more, spend more, produce more, contribute more, and know more, and therefore we demand more," Tomsson Black said, "but despite the fact we have grown in numbers, we haven't grown comparably in wealth. And this is a capitalistic nation, where all life forces derive from wealth. We know this, but most of the wealth of the nation belongs to white people, and as a consequence they control the destiny of our nation. Therefore we protest the unfairness of this. We want our share of the nation's wealth so we can control our own destinies. But that does not mean we hate white people. We have too much to love you for."

It was this outburst that finally broke down Mr. Hopkins' reserve and began to swing the pendulum in Tomsson Black's favor. What had at first been intended for two or three brief interviews at the most, turned into long daily discussions touching upon many topics. Hopkins' greatest interest was in Tomsson Black's opinions on what steps blacks had taken to adapt to a way of life that was principally designed by whites and for whites.

"In most instances we can do no more than imitate," Tomsson Black confessed. "We have so little tradition outside the structure of our national society, that we have very few basic innovations to offer. With the exception of jazz music, I do not know of a single contribution we have made to American life from our racial heritage. Of course, there are habits and customs we acquired from our tenure of slavery that have, in recent years, become popularized. But most of them were adapted from the whites and forced upon us for the purpose of survival, such as soul food and spirituals. However, soul food came from vegetables and animals the whites raise for their own food, and merely consisted of the parts they threw away.

"We have taken our language from the whites, our knowledge and education from the whites, our morals and religions from the whites, our definitions of justice, ambition, achievement, clothing, shelter; in fact every aspect of our lives but reproduction, which is common to all life. We do not have any remembered tradition. What we know of the African life of our ancestors comes from information recorded by whites. Even Africans themselves are dependant on these white records to learn of their own past. It is not a question of whether we should adapt to the way of life created by whites for whites, since there is no other way of life to which we can adapt.

"And if we create a way of life for ourselves, the very act

of this creation will be an imitation of that of the whites. Whatever tradition the blacks ever had on earth is gone and transplanted by the civilization the whites have imposed on the earth, and it is highly unlikely we would want to go back and live like our ancestors, even if we could. But many admirable tendencies have come from this paradoxical attitude of ours. We have learned that to us, black is beautiful. But this, too, we have learned from the whites, who began terming themselves beautiful when they first began to rule the world. All people in authority must, of a necessity, be beautiful. God is beautiful. All rulers are beautiful. Power endows one with beauty. It is not only natural but essential that people of all races must be beautiful to themselves. We blacks in the U. S. have ignored this obvious fact, for, in the acquisition of all of our other cultural attributes from whites, we have accepted their definition of beauty, too."

"Black people are beautiful, too," Hopkins said.

"Of course, sir," said Tomsson Black. "That is what I've been saying. 'Too' is the operative word. We are human, too; we are intelligent, too; we are worthy, too; but we are not white, too, and that is the problem. We are everything but white in a white-dominated, white-oriented society. The one thing which we lack is white skin. So we must imitate the dominant group, as has every minority group in the history of the world. Unlike most minority groups, however, when we achieve our imitation even to perfection, we can not move over into the majority group and become assimilated because of the barrier of our skin. That makes us different from almost all other minority groups through-out history.

"We must achieve our equality in this society against overwhelming odds. That is why we need a springboard, why we need a beginning. We need capital. The white people had slaves, the wedding of coal and ore, the unlim-ited grazing plains, the fertile earth, the gold rush, the underground lakes of petroleum. With all that, it didn't require too much creative imagination for this nation to be-come rich and prosperous. We, however, must start at the bottom, at the chitterling of the hog. We don't own fertile fields and slaves to till them for us, we own no plains, we're too late for the gold rush, we own no oil-bearing land. We own only ourselves, and we can't even hire ourselves out to the highest bidder, which is another privilege of the white man. We must take what we are offered for ourselves, and oftimes that is very little. Of course, we are beautiful, too, but that will get us very little of the capital we so badly need, and it might very well hinder us."

"If it were up to me, I would see that black people were given equal rights this instant," Hopkins said sincerely. Lapsing into pragmatic self-derogation, he added, "But no one ever has the will or the authority to act against the will of the majority. Not even dictators," he concluded after a moment's comtemplation.

"I am not requesting you to act alone," Tomsson Black said. "I hope to persuade the majority of our nation's white people that this project is in their own best interests."

The interrogation did not end there. Mr. Hopkins felt that he owned it to his employer, the Hull Foundation, and the whole of the white majority nation, to explore every facet of this man's mind before granting him the power that he requested. For if this project was to be a success, it would be the first concrete example of black power in the history of the nation. So he kept probing at Tomsson Black's mind until it seemed at times that it afforded him some sadistic pleasure.

"Tell me, Mr. Black, what was your honest opinion of Dr. Martin Luther King?"

"I thought Dr. King was the greatest man who ever lived. I thought he was concerned not only with the welfare of us black people, but with the moral character of the nation as a whole. I thought he was a selfless leader, and I particularly admired his stand against violence. I thought his death was a loss to all men of character in the world, regardless of race, creed, color, or political ideology."

Mr. Hopkins nodded. "I find that we agree, as we have on so many varied subjects. Dr. King was a man among men. And what is your opinion of Roy Wilkins?"

For an instant the name did not register in Tomsson Black's memory. It was as though, unconsciously, he suffered from a block. But suddenly his memory cleared and he smiled with relief.

"I grew up with the feeling that Mr. Wilkins, as the head of the NAACP, was the titular leader of our race, and as such, I automatically admired his wisdom and intelligence and took it for granted that he always acted in our best interests.

"Mmmm, but you have not stated your own private, unrehearsed opinion of Mr. Wilkins," Hopkins said.

"I thought I had, sir. I think he is an intelligent and wise leader. He does not have the personal magnetism, the charisma, that Dr. King possessed, but he is a wise and perceptive leader of our people."

"And Malcolm X? What was your opinion of Malcolm X? I believe you were personally acquainted with him."

"No, my father knew him but I never met him. All I know of Malcolm X is what my father said, what I have read of him and what he wrote about himself in his autobiography."

"And what was that?"

"My father was a great admirer of Malcolm X, but I could never understand the logic that made him anti-white. Of course, he grew out of it as he developed, but that was what my father most admired about him."

"Is your father anti-white?"

"He was, sir."

"You say 'was,' then I take it he is dead."

"He was killed in an accident the year before Malcolm X was assassinated."

"And is your mother still alive?"

"No sir, she died six years ago when I was abroad."

"Do you think the loss of your father affected your subsequent life?"

"There is no doubt about it, sir," Tomsson Black said. "But I have always felt that its effect was more constructive than adverse. It conditioned me to think for myself and bear the blame for my mistakes instead of trying to shift it onto others. Of a necessity, I had to be self-reliant. I had always to analyze my attitudes and reexamine my decisions. Because of this, despite all my mistakes, I grew and gravitated toward the light. That is the one thing for which Malcolm X won my unadulterated admiration. He never stopped growing.

"He grew from a juvenile life of crime and hatred to become a leader of black people," Tomsson Black continued. "It is true that he took some of the hatred with him but he was strong enough to grow out of it. When he was assassinated, he loved all people of all races, despite their shortcomings. I would say that both he and Dr. King had arrived at the ultimate point in their love for humanity, although by quite different roads, by the time they were assassinated."

"Tell me, Mr. Black, did you feel—believe—a conspiracy was involved in either of these assassinations?"

"Mr. Hopkins, as a black man my emotional reaction to both these assassinations was highly partisan and chauvinistic. I wanted to believe that both of these irreplacable leaders were victims of conspiracies of white racists. I wanted to believe this. I wanted so badly to believe it that, to accept the proof of public evidence, the judgement of white jurists and the dictates of my own reason to the opposite conclusion, was one of the hardest struggles of my life. One of the privileges that white people have that we don't is their privilege to think what we dare not."

And so it went, day after day, with Mr. Hopkins probing into Tomsson Black's mind and Tomsson Black struggling with all his skill and eloquence to defend his identity. Time and again, when it was least expected, Hopkins would question Tomsson Black's reaction to his imprisonment for rape, and oftimes he would pose the question of an imposed sense of guilt. Can one avoid a sense of guilt for a crime one has committed, whether he has paid the prescribed debt to society or not? And each time Tomsson Black would reiterate that he no longer felt a sense of guilt for a crime he had paid for.

"I was justly accused and sentenced," he would repeat. "I paid my debt to society without complaint. I do not think nor feel that I should keep on paying my debt to society through a sense of guilt. The original meaning of the word penitentiary implied the absolution of sin and the end of penitence. My penitence ended when I was freed from the penitentiary. I believe that Mr. and Mrs. Goodfeller will support this attitude. Whether they do or not, I am stuck with it, sir. If I still suffered from a sense of guilt I would not be in your office now. I would not have had the vision to conceive this project, nor the necessary assurance to activate it."

"Mr. Black, I must commend you on the eloquence of your appeal," Hopkins said drily. "I am inclined to think that if you had pled your own case in court, you would not have been convicted."

"I thank God I was," Tomsson Black said passionately. "It was through my imprisonment that I came to see the light."

Then as last, Hopkins asked Tomsson Black if he had any objection to being psychoanalized.

It was Tomsson Black's turn to smile. "Why, do you think I am crazy, sir?"

"Not at all, Mr. Black. But there are people in this world who would think you were, if you walked into their office and asked them for a million dollars, for whatever purpose."

"I am well aware of that, sir. But I felt from the beginning that the potential benefits to my people outweighed the risks of any adverse opinion of me."

"Well said, and I assure you that I think you are one of the least crazy persons I have ever met. But I'm curious what your subconscious will reveal about your loyalty and your true attitude toward white people. You have expressed your conscious attitudes on these subjects—and very eloquently. Now I would like to know if your subconscious attitudes will be the same."

"I would like to know, too, sir," Tomsson Black said ironically.

However, the discovery of these subconscious attitudes was not to take place. Mr. Hopkins succumbed to a heart attack shortly after signing the order to pay to Chitterlings, Inc. the sum of one million dollars.

CHAPTER 21

The police parade was headed north up the main street of the big city. Of the thirty thousand policemen employed by the big city, six thousand were in the parade. It had been billed as a parade of unity to demonstrate the strength of law enforcement and reassure the "communities" during this time of suspicion and animosity between the races. No black policemen were parading for the simple reason that none of them had been asked to parade, and none of them had requested the right.

At no time had the races been so utterly divided, despite the billing of unity given to the parade. Judging from both the appearances of the paraders and the viewers lining the street, the word "unity" seemed more applicable than the diffident allusion to the "races." Only the white race was on view, and it seemed perfectly unified. In fact, the crowd of white faces seemed to deny that a black race existed.

The police commissioner and the chiefs of the various police departments under him led the parade. They were white. The captains of the precinct stations followed, and the lieutenants in charge of the precinct detective bureaus, and the uniformed patrolmen followed them. They were all white, as were all of the plainclothes detectives and uniformed patrolmen who made up the bulk of the parade following. All white. As were the spectators behind the police cordons lining the main street of the big city. As were all the people employed on that street in department stores and office buildings who crowded to doors and windows to watch the police parade pass.

⟨There was only one black man along the entire length of the street at the time, and he wasn't in sight.⟩ He was standing in a small, unlighted chamber to the left of the entrance to the big city's large Catholic cathedral on the main street. As a rule, this chamber held the poor box, from which the daily donations were collected by a preoccupied priest in the service of the cathedral at six p. m. each day. Now it was shortly past three o'clock and there were almost three hours before collection time. The only light in the dark room came through two slots where the donations were made, one in the stone front wall that opened on to the street, and the other through the wooden door that opened into the vestibule. The door was locked and the black man had the chamber to himself.

Chutes ran down from the slots into a closed coin box on legs. The black man had removed the chutes which restricted his movements, and he now could sit straddling the coin box. The slot in the stone front wall gave him a clear view of the street up which the policemen's parade would march. Beside him on the floor was a cold bottle of lemon-ade collecting beads of sweat in the hot, humid air. In his arms he held a blued-steel automatic rifle of the type that had been employed by other black men to slaughter whites. He did not think of them; they were dead. He was only concerned with the living.

The muzzle of the barrel rested on the inner edge of the slot in the stone wall and was invisible from without. He sat patiently, as though he had all the time in the world, waiting for the parade to come into sight. He had all the rest of his life. He had waited four hundred years for this moment and he was not in a hurry. They would come, he knew, and he would be waiting for them.

He knew his black people would suffer severely for this moment of his triumph. He was not an ignorant man. Although he mopped the floors and polished the pews of this white cathedral, he was not without intelligence. He knew the whites would kill him, too. It was almost as though he were already dead. It required a mental effort to keep from making the sign of the cross, but he knew the God of this cathedral was white and would have no tolerance for him. And there was no black God nearby, if in fact there was one anywhere in the U. S.

Now, at the end of his life, he would have to rely on himself. He would have to assume the authority that controlled his life. He would have to direct his will that directed his brain that directed his finger to pull the trigger. He would have to do it alone, without comfort or encouragement, consoled only by the hope that it would make life safer for blacks in the future. He would have to believe that although blacks would suffer now, there would be those who would benefit later. He would have to hope that whites would have a second thought when they knew it was their own blood being wasted. This decision he would have to make alone. He would have to control his thoughts in order to formulate the thought he wanted. There was no one to shape the thought for him. This is the way it should have been all along, to make the decision, to think for himself, to die without supplication. If his death was in vain, and whites would never accept blacks as equal human beings, there was nothing to live for anyway.

Through the slot in the stone front wall of the cathedral, he saw the first row of the long police parade come into view. He could faintly hear the martial music of the band that was still out of sight. In the front row, a tall, sallow-skinned man with gray hair, wearing a gray civilian suit, white shirt and black tie, walked in the center of four red-faced, gold-braided police chiefs. The black man did not know enough about the police organization to identify the police departments from the uniforms of the chiefs, but he recognized the man in the civilian suit as the police com-missioner. He had seen photographs of him in the news-paper. The commissioner wore highly-polished spectacles with black frames that glinted in the rays of the afternoon sun, but the frosty blue eyes of the chief inspectors, squint-ing in the sun, were without aids.

The black man's muscles tightened, a tremor ran through his body. This was it. He lifted his rifle, but they had to march slightly further before he could get them in his sights. He had waited this long, he could wait a few seconds longer.

The first burst, passing from left to right, made a row of entries in the faces of the five officers in the lead. The first officers were of the same height, and holes appeared in their upper cheekbones, just beneath the eyes and in the bridges of their noses. Snot mixed with blood exploded from their nostrils and their caps flew off behind, suddenly filled with fragments of their skulls and pasty gray brain matter, slightly interlaced with capillaries, like gobs of putty, finely-sculpted with red ink.

The commissioner, who was slightly shorter, was hit in both temples and both eyes, and the bullets made star-shaped entries in both the lenses of his spectacles and the corners of his eyeballs, and a gelatinous substance heavily mixed with blood spurted from the rims of his eyesockets. He wore no hat to catch his brains, and fragments of skull. They exploded through the sunny atmosphere and splattered the spectators with gooey, bloody brain matter, tufts of gray hair, and splinters of skull.

One skull fragment, larger than the others, struck a tall, well-dressed man on the cheek, cutting the skin and splashing brains against his face like a custard pie in a Max Sennet comedy.

The two chiefs on the far side, being a shade taller than

the others, caught the bullets in their teeth. These latter suffered worse, if such a thing was possible. Bloodstained teeth flew through the air like exotic insects. A shattered denture was expelled forward from the shattered jaw like the puking of plastic food. Jawbones came unhinged and dangled from shattered mouths. But the ultimate damage was that the heads were cut off just above the bottom jaws, which swung grotesquely from headless bodies that spouted blood like gory fountains.

The scene was made eerie by fact that the gunshots could not be heard over the blasting of the band and the sound-proof walls of the cathedral. The heads of five men were shattered to bits, without a sound and for no reason that was immediately apparent. It was uncanny. Pandemonium reigned. No one knew which way to run from the unseen danger, so everyone ran in every direction. Men, women, and children dashed about panickstricken, screaming, their blue eyes popping or squinting, their mouths open or their teeth gritting, their faces paper-white or lobster-red.

The brave policemen in the lines behind their slaughtered commissioner and chiefs drew their pistols and rapped out orders. Captains and lieutenants were bellowing to the plainclothes detectives and uniformed patrolmen in the ranks at the rear to come forward and do their duty. Row after row of captains and lieutenants were shot down with their service revolvers in their hands. After the first burst, the black man had lowered his sights and was now shooting the captains in the abdomen, riddling hearts and lungs, livers and kidneys, bursting pot bellies like paper sacks of water.

In a matter of seconds, the streets were strewn with the carnage. Nasty gray blobs of brains, hairy fragments of skull looking like exotic sections of broken coconuts, bone splinters from jaws, facial bones, bloody, gristly bits of ears and noses, flying red and white teeth, a section of tongue, and slick and slimy with large, purpling splashes and gouts of blood. There were squashy bits of exploded viscera, stuffed intestines bursting with half-chewed ham and cabbage and rice and gravy, lying in the gutters like unfinished sausages before knotting. Scattered about in this bloody carnage were what remained of the bodies of policemen, still clad in blood-clotted blue uniforms.

Spectators were killed purely by accident. They were caught in the line of fire by bullets that had already passed through their intended victims. It was revealing that most of these were clean, comely matrons snugly fitting into their smooth white skins, and little girl children with long blonde braids.

Whether from reflex or design, most mature men and little boys had ducked for cover, flattening themselves to the pavement or rolling into doorways and underneath parked cars in much the same way the blacks had done up on Eighth Avenue during the gun fight between the lone black killer and the police.

Unlike that duel in the dark, the black man now behind the gun had not yet been seen nor had his hiding place been discovered. The front doors of the cathedral were closed and the stained glass windows high up on the front wall were sealed. The slot in the wall for donations to charity was barely visible from the street and then only if the gaze deliberately sought it out. It was shaded by the architecture of the clerestory so that the dulled blued-steel gun barrel didn't glint in the sun. As a consequence, the brave policemen with their service revolvers in their hands were running helter-skelter with nothing to shoot at while being mown down by the black killer.

The white spectators were fortunate that there were no blacks among them, for had these irate, nervous cops spied a black face in their midst, there was no calculating the number of whites who would have been accidentally killed by them. However, all were decided, police and spectators alike, that the sniper was a black man, since no one else would slaughter whites so wantonly, like a sadist stomping on an ant hill.

In view of the history of all the assassinations and mass murders in the U. S., it was extraordinarily enlightening that the thousands of white police and civilians would automatically agree that he must be black. Had they always experienced such foreboding? Was it a pathological portent? Was it inherited? Was it constant, like original sin? Was it a presentiment of the times? Who knows? The whites had always been as secretive of their fears and failings as had the blacks.

But it was the most gratifying episode of the black man's

life. He experienced an intensity of feeling akin to sexual ecstasy when he saw the brains flying from those white men's heads and fat, arrogant white bodies shattered and cast into death. Hate served his pleasure. He thought fleetingly and pleasurably of all the humiliations and hurts imposed on him and all other blacks by whites. The outrage of slavery flashed across his mind and he could see whites with a strange, pure clarity, eating the flesh of blacks. He knew at last that they were the only real cannibals who had ever existed.

He felt only indifference when he saw the riot tank come rushing up the wide main street from police headquarters to kill him. He was so far ahead that they could never get even now, he thought. He drew in the barrel of his gun to keep his position from being revealed and waited patiently for his death. He was ready to die, because by then he had killed seventy-three whites, forty-seven policemen, and twenty-six men, women, and children civilians, and had wounded an additional seventy-five. Although he would never know the true score, he was satisfied. He felt like a gambler who has broken the bank. He knew they would kill him quickly, but that was satisfactory, too.

Astonishingly enough, though, there remained a few moments of macabre comedy before his death arrived. The riot tank didn't know where to look for him. Its telescoped eye at the muzzle of the 105 mm cannon stared right and left, looking over the heads of the white spectators and the living white policemen as they hopped about the dead who lay all up and down the main street with its impressive storefronts. The cannon seemed frustrated at not seeing a black face to shoot at, and began to shoot explosive shells at the black plaster-of-paris mannequins in a display of beach wear in a department store window.

The concussion was devastating. Splintered plate glass filled the air like a sand storm. Faces were split open and lacerated by flying glass splinters. One woman's head was cut completely off by a piece of flying glass as large as a guillotine. Varicolored wigs flew from white heads like frightened long-haired birds taking flight. Many other men, women, and children were stripped stark naked by the force of the concussion.

Seeing bits of black mannequin sailing past, a rookie cop thought the blacks were attacking from the sky and loosed a fusilade from his .38 calibre police special. With a reflex that appeared shockingly human, the tank whirled about and blasted two 105 mm shells into the already panic-stricken policemen, instantly blowing twenty-nine of them to bits and wounding another one hundred and seventeen with flying shrapnel.

By then, the screaming had grown so loud that suddenly all motion ceased, as though a valve in the heart had stopped. With the cessation of motion, silence fell like a pall. Springing out of this motionless silence, a teen-aged boy ran across the blood-slick streets and pointed with his slender arm and delicate hand at the coin slot in the cathedral. All heads pivoted in that direction as though on a common neck, and the tank turned to stare at the stone wall with its eye, also. But no sign of life was visible against the blank stone wall and the heavy, brass-studded wooden doors. The tank seemed to stare for a moment, as if in deep thought, then 105 mm cannon shells began to rain upon the stone. People fled from the flying debris. It did not take very long for the cannon to reduce the stone face of the cathedral to a pile of rubbish. However, it took most of the following day to unearth the twisted rifle and a few scraps of bloody flesh that proved a black killer had existed. In the wake of this bloody massacre, the stock market crashed. The dollar fell on the world market. The very structure of capitalism began to crumble. Confidence in the capitalistic system had an almost fatal shock. All over the world, millions of capitalists sought means to invest their wealth in the communist east.

CHAPTER 22

The reaction of whites to the massacre in front of the cathedral was of such murderous intensity that the very structure of their civilization was threatened. The white community had previously accused the police of overreacting to these black killers, but now it was the community, itself, that overreacted, and seemed to take a thorough enjoyment in it.

There was an immediate outcry demanding the use of the armed forces to exterminate the black race, but on second thought, the whites realized that this would deprive them of all menial labor. Who would collect the garbage, mop the floors, wash the dishes, mow the lawns, chop the cotton and hoe the corn? That wouldn't do at all, they reasoned. But what if only the males were exterminated? Better still, what if all black males were castrated? That would drain them of their aggressive tendencies and, at the same time, leave them physically capable of performing all menial chores.

Naturally the armed forces could not debase themselves by performing this act, so various individual racists went ahead with the idea, and offered a bounty for every set of black testicles that were delivered. However, this did not prove very rewarding, since no black male was found willing to stand still while being deprived of his testicles.

Frustrated in their endeavor to create a race of eunuchs, a thing that would have relieved white males of the inferiority they felt from the black males' larger penises, whites next advocated the re-establishment of the institution of slavery.

There was a lot to be said for black slavery, despite the opinions of Lincoln and the Abolitionists, they decided, after an interval of sober thought. Black slaves had been kept in hunger and ignorance, as helpless as knocked-up and barefooted Irish women. After all, white slave owners had had nothing to fear but the envy and fanaticism of other whites. Not only would slavery establish blacks in a permanent condition of animalism and servitude, but it would comply with their demands for meaningful employment and fulfill their desire for separation. The whites were soon to learn, though, that slavery was no longer feasible. Nowhere in modern architecture had allowance been made for the necessity of slave cabins.

Whites became infuriated at the frustrations they found at every turn. No eunuchs, no slaves, and as yet, blacks had not yet been punished. There was a sudden outbreak of lynching all over the nation, north-south-east-west. Black males were lynched on sight, at busy intersections of main streets in broad daylight, on lonely roads near large farms and ranches, in their own remote and desolate share-cropper shacks. They were lynched in every imaginable manner. Alongside the traditional hanging-and-burning, there were modern innovations. Some were crushed against walls by large, powerful cars. Some were chopped to death by women's stiletto heels. Some were drenched with gasoline and set afire and let free to run and fan the flames. Some were simply beaten to death by whatever blunt instruments were close to hand.

To keep alive, black males went underground. They went Ellison to live wherever they felt they would be out of sight of the whites. Their ghetto tenements were periodically invaded by the police and were consequently considered unsafe. Even the basements and cellars of their tenements were not considered safe from the relentless police pursuit and their armies of informers. These places were also just as likely to prove death traps during the systematic searches for guns.

So they went outside of the ghettos to go underground. At first, the favorite underground hiding places, made appealing by black writers, were the sewers and conduits for the various public services, such as electricity, telephones, water, steam, and the like. These places honeycombed the areas beneath the buildings of every large city and were easily reached by numerous manholes.

But these places had various drawbacks, which black males soon discovered. It was difficult and dangerous for black females to bring them food. Any female caught passing a pot of hopping john down a manhole to an unseen recipient was immediately suspect. Because these places had been so highly publicized by the black writers who had made them seem so appealing to blacks, they were consequently one of the first places the whites looked for them.

But blacks were not without their own power. Many of them had taken the dangerous, illicit rifles that they had received into hiding with them. They proved almost invulnerable as they sniped from beneath slightly raised manhole covers. Even the riot tanks were ineffective against these forays. Only bombing was entirely effective, and because so many manholes were located in densely-populated business districts, the bombs had to be limited in size and delivered by midget helicopters, which, themselves, easily fell prey to black sniper fire. Nevertheless, the number of bombs successfully dropped on manholes was sufficient to pit the streets of the big cities like the face of the moon.

Soon, blacks who did not have guns began to take pipe cutters and wire cutters and small acetylene torches with them into hiding so they could cut water pipes, and telephone and electric cables, thereby sabotaging the communications and sanitation of the cities. Highly sensitive and important areas of economic, cultural, and commercial activity, such as Wall Street and Rockefeller Center, suddenly found themselves without water, lights, and telephones. Thousands of people were trapped in elevators, some of whom died of heart failure. Others committed suicide and a few went mad and killed the others.

Tycoons had their telephone conversations cut when they heard the sound "F . . . ," in the middle of million dollar business deals. They had to sweat it out for hours before learning whether they had been told "Fine," or "Fuck you." Executives were suddenly plunged into black darkness at just the moments they were about to plunge their stiff "boonies" into their secretaries' wet "moonies," and instead felt them striking against all sorts of unexpected hazards and even straying into such unlikely things as inkwells, paper cups, and waste baskets. And the absence of water, of course, led to dirty hands, the malfunctioning of plumbing, the discouragement of loitering in the johns, and the pervading, astonishingly permissive odor of shit.

But the continual bombing of manholes influenced many blacks to seek less obvious and more permanent hiding places where they could receive food and have their women visit them, or else do it to each other in comparative privacy and security. They began to move into less obvious places, such as the basements of commercial buildings, storage warehouses, and the isolated housings of dynamos that were protected with the warning, "DANGER! KEEP OUT!"

White custodians and specialized workers were startled out of their wits upon coming face to face with vaguely-seen blacks in dimly-lit, unlikely places. Some were slain outright, silently strangled. Some dropped dead of fright. Others found themselves seized and their throats and vocal cords bitten out by large, dangerous teeth. Soon it reached the point where no white man was willing to enter a dark, uninhabited area alone, not even his own basement to stoke the furnace.

It was then that a lunatic fringe of white racists organized gangs of vigilantes to hunt the blacks out of their holes as though they were wild beasts. Safaris of hunters armed with hunting guns searched the cities for underground outlets where they could smoke the blacks out and shoot them. At the same time, white women armed themselves with handguns to protect their homes in case a wild black got loose.

But the blacks proved to be more dangerous than jungle beasts. They were more intelligent and they had knowledge and experience of the cities. They were the mental equal of whites and were better armed. Living in the ghettoes had made them immune to smoke and stinking gases and they just stayed put in their underground holes, waiting for the whites to come in after them.

So what at first had been a vigilante action was now the most dangerous and exciting of all sports. It became known all over the civilized world as "THE BLACK HUNT." Unlike the other game killed by civilized hunters, it was not necessary to give blacks any advantage to even the odds. The black was more cunning than his white counterpart, faster moving, and could run faster and jump further. He was strong and agile, and danger enhanced his frenzy. And above all, when stripped naked, he was almost invisible in the dark.

The element of danger attracted all of the famous white hunters in the world, both professionals with big-game experience who were employed to organize these new safaris, and the millionare sportsmen grown jaded with shooting insipid lions and tigers, dull-whitted water buffalo, clumsy rhinoceri, and the too-too vulnerable elephants.

Even famous American millionare philanthropists, known for their advocacy of equal civil rights, who deplored the killing of bulls by toreadors, hare by hounds, horses by butchers, and who at first had been repulsed and outraged by this inhuman manhunt, eventually succumbed to the sheer entrancement of hunting niggers instead of having to hire them, and to the inexpressible exhuberance of bagging a big dangerous black buck and cutting off his testicles to have them mounted in the trophy room.

Shortly the greatest hunters alive were engaged in THE BLACK HUNT! Master trackers, schools of beaters, white hunters, blonde nymphomaniacs, and whites with so little knowledge of this most masculine of all sports that they had to brush up on old stories by Hemingway to learn what position to take with their wives.

But still the blacks proved formidable, and if a white hunter dropped his guard for just an instant, he was felled by a right cross to the jaw.

CHAPTER 23

Needless to say, the presidential administration was appalled by this deterioration of civilized morality. A conference was called of all members of the cabinet, Supreme Court, leaders of Congress, and white civic leaders who had kept aloof from the exciting sport, to discuss ways and means of putting an end to this barbaric immorality. It was suggested that the blacks should first agree to quit massacring whites before any further committment was made, for after all, the actions of the whites were merely retaliatory. This had the appeal of first convicting blacks before pleading the mercy of the whites, as was the traditional custom, and was agreed upon by all present.

But how were blacks to be made to stop massacring the whites, especially in view of their aversion to "THE BLACK HUNT?"

Spontaneously, the name of Tomsson Black, the young black president of Chitterlings, Inc., the only black male still free to come and go as he pleased, sprang to everyone's mind. Tomsson Black, they argued, was the only black who commanded sufficient admiration and trust of other blacks to insure that the plan was listened to. What was more, the whites trusted him, too.

As soon as it was learned that Tomsson Black would appeal to his black brothers to abandon those homicidal impulses which led only to death and disgrace, all of the major television and radio networks, independant stations, local and national and international newspapers and news magazines, all the various media of communications, offered him time and space. The television networks gave him their most effective hour between seven and eight p. m., at the cost of millions of dollars in advertising revenue. The news magazines put his picture on all of their covers and, when he consented to the conference's request, newspapers carried headlines in type the size customarily employed to announce a world war:

TOMSSON BLACK SPEAKS TO THE NATION.

The gist of Tomsson Black's appeal was for blacks to count their blessings, to know their friends, to be orderly and law-abiding, to trust their government and do the right thing.

No one in the white community thought this cornpone, slavery-time gibberish was strange language for an appeal to insane, homicidal blacks in the last half of the twentieth century. It had worked wonderfully for them for more than a century, so why shouldn't it work for Tomsson Black, who had won the respect and admiration of his people. Furthermore, no sane white person was capable of believing that a sane black person might have a deep-seated homicidal hatred for them.

As a consequence, the white community was amazed beyond measure when black men still kept running amok and killing white people with foreign guns.

EDITORS' NOTE: No formal conclusion exists for Plan B. The following pages are reconstructed from a detailed outline found with the rest of the manuscript.

It was then that the Establishment decided to send trusted black men underground to track down the source of the guns. Grave Digger's suspension was lifted and he was ordered to return to duty with Coffin Ed by Captain Brice.

"Now I want you fellows to get yourselves fired," the captain instructed them.

"How?" Grave Digger asked. "I thought I was already fired."

"Hell, you ought to know how to get yourself fired," the captain said. "Take a bribe from a pusher; wreck a police car while you're off duty; get in a brawl downtown outside of your precinct; libel the commissioner—"

"How about beating up on some brothers' heads?"

"Hell, you know we woudn't fire you for that—not really. But you'll find a way, I'm sure," the captain ventured.

"All right, we get fired. Then what?" Digger asked.

"I'll spread the story, get it in the papers, on TV. Everybody'll know in a week's time. Of course, you'll still be on the payroll, you understand that?"

"Yeah, we understand," Digger answered.

"Get around the bars, the shooting galleries, the whore houses. With a couple of tough hoods like you boys on the loose, somebody's bound to contact you," the captain said. "Play it cool, talk anti-white, let the contact lead. Sooner or later, somebody's gonna want two boys like you with your big, fast guns. Just keep in touch and buzz me what you find out."

"We hear you, boss," Digger said. "Sound just like a hipster. When we find something to spiel, we'll buzz you, boss."

In a couple of days, they dropped into Small's Bar during the afternoon. Everybody there knew they had been fired for taking a bribe from the Syndicate's Harlem connection, but no one said a word.

From then on, they hung around pool rooms, bars, shooting galleries, prostitution pads. They acted resentful and ill-used. They gave a very creditable performance of having a hard-on for whitey, of being so anti-white that they wouldn't drink a white cow's milk. They were charged with several assaults against white people, and it became common knowledge that they had beaten many whites mercilessly and had never been caught.

Their behavior was in character and therefore believable. They had worked for the establishment as hatchet men on their race, had kissed the white man's ass, and now that they were considered no longer useful and had been thrown out in the street, they had turned on him with hatred and resentment, venomous and murderous like blind snakes in the heat of August.

However, they didn't find out any more about the source of the guns than was already known. By accident they had caught one of the delivery boys who had just delivered a gun and they tortured him unmercifully, trying to make him talk. Either he didn't know where the gun had come from or else he was resolved to die before he told. He was hospitalized in time for his life to be saved and, surprisingly, the black cops-turned vicious hoodlums escaped punishment. No one identified them, no one testified against them.

In talking it over between themselves, they discovered that each had become convinced, of his own accord, that the only organization of the right size, with enough resources, and with the right contacts in the black community necessary for the acquisition and distribution of the guns was the firm of Chitterlings, Inc.

They contacted Lieutenant Anderson and told him they had something to report. He asked if they had any facts, forcing them to confess that all they had was a theory.

It took Anderson some time to convince the brass to listen to the theory, but they finally agreed to listen. The two black detectives waxed eloquent in their charge that Chitterlings, Inc. was the only organization in all the world that fitted the bill. Hadn't its founder and president formerly belonged to all of the militant, anti-white groups in the U. S.? Hadn't he founded the Big Blacks? Hadn't he castigated the police? Hadn't he visited all the anti-American capitols of the communist world? Wasn't he the only U. S. black anarchist who had had the opportunity to learn about guerilla war from the leading revolutionaries of the world? If the guns were not being distributed by Tomsson Black through Chitterlings, Inc., then the entire episode was a figment of the imagination, they argued.

The police commissioner looked at the district attorney. The chief of the New York office of the FBI nodded toward an official of the CIA.

The CIA official admitted that they had had Tomsson Black under suspicion since the start. They had reviewed his entire career; they had sent agents to many communist capitols to investigate his former activities. There was nothing about his entire life, from the cradle, that the CIA didn't know. And in this case, they were forced to give him a clean bill of health. They had discovered no firm evidence, nor even a suspicion of a connection, between his activities and the distribution of the guns. Their detailed investigation only confirmed their belief that he had had a complete change of heart from his former anti-white period, that he was now a firm and staunch supporter of law, order, and the American way, and that he was as trustworthy a black man as it was possible to find.

The FBI official admitted that they had also thoroughly investigated the firm of Chitterlings, Inc. from both the inside and the outside. They had traced its formation, discovered and interviewed all the original backers, examined its articles of incorporation, interviewed a cross-section of its personnel, and contacted individually all the known police informers who had ever been in its employ. None of them admitted to knowing any more about the guns than what they had read in the newspapers.

The only incident that the FBI found interesting involved a ten-thousand-ton freighter that had become incapacitated in Mobile Bay on the night of the last December 24th. At 4:03 A. M., December 25th, the freighter had broadcast an SOS. Witnesses later testified that they had seen heavy black smoke coming from below and enveloping the upper decks. At 4:15 A. M., radio contact had been made with the Coast Guard in Mobile Bay and a Coast Guard cutter had been quickly dispatched to its rescue. The sleepy crew of the cutter had scarcely retired from Christmas Eve celebrations and it was with an ill will that they set forth into the cold, gloomy morning. By the time they arrived at the disabled freighter, the fire in its engine room had been checked. However, the engines had been damaged beyond repair.

The freighter was flying the Liberian flag but was leased by a textile industry in Hong Kong. The captain and mate were Chinese, the crew a mixture of other Orientals of many varying nationalities. It had delivered a consignment of silk worms with all the necessary food-producing trees and plants for their existence, along with a number of Asiatic experts to supervise their care and propagation in Havana for the Cuban government, which had embarked upon a project of native silk production for its own textile industry. When the fire had broken out, the ship had been enroute to the port of New Orleans to pick up a consignment of raw cotton for manufacturers in Hong Kong.

The Chinese skipper, who appeared to be thoroughly Anglicized, admitted that they had been rushing to New Orleans, hoping to be there in time for a Christmas Eve celebration when a boiler had become overheated and caught on fire.

The Coast Guard cutter's captain examined the freighter's papers and found them in order. However, the Coast Guard crew were aggravated by the nationality of the captain and his mate, despite their English courtesy, so they made quick work of towing the freighter into drydock in Mobile Bay, from which it wouldn't be able to put to sea again until the first week in January.

However, thorough investigation proved that not one of the personnel of Chitterlings, Inc.'s main plant nearby had ever heard of the disabled freighter in Mobile Bay.

So the FBI was in complete accord with the CIA that Chitterlings, Inc. and its president, Tomsson Black, could be declared free of all suspicion.

The district attorney pointedly suggested that black people who tried to publicize unfounded suspicions against Tomsson Black and Chitterlings, Inc. could only be considered as suspect themselves.

The commissioner admitted that he was personally acquainted with Tomsson Black, who had impressed him as a thoroughly loyal and dependable and patriotic black American who had proved beyond all doubt that he was completely rehabilitated.

Captain Brice admitted, "I'd trust him, too. I'd always thought that he was bought."

The conversation continued in this vein until the white conferees became so incensed at the black detectives for suspecting their boy, Tomsson Black, that the commissioner dismissed them from the force for real and denied them any benefits from the police pension agency.

Afterward Grave Digger said, "We should have our heads examined. Even a black child knows better than to suspect a white man's favorite nigger."

"Funny enough," Coffin Ed conceded. "Them's the only mother rapers who can get away with anything."

"Yeah, whitey'll trust them when he won't even trust himself.

They were out of their jobs again, but there was something different about it this time. This was for real and the black brothers sensed it.

The two ex-detectives were arrested for wearing their pistols, which they had worn ever since they had been on the force. Now, however, the pistols are considered concealed weapons. They were taken down to the precinct station by white cops and charged under the Sullivan Act.

Soon a strange black woman appeared, and went bail for

the two of them. She was so sexy that at first Grave Digger and Coffin Ed thought she was a high-class hooker looking for a bodyguard. She asked them if they wanted to work for their race and told them that Tomsson Black wanted to talk with them.

She took them to her home in White Plains, where they found Tomsson Black waiting. In an atmosphere of assured privacy, Tomsson Black told the ex-cops that he was greatly concerned about the guns that were continuing to fall into the hands of black maniacs. He wanted to employ them to find out where the guns were coming from.

"That's what the white man wanted," Grave Digger admitted.

"And you couldn't find out?" Tomsson Black asked.

"Oh, we found out," Digger answered.

"Why didn't you tell him?"

"We did."

"What happened?"

"He fired us."

"Do you object to telling me?"

"No."

"Who, then?"

"You."

Tomsson Black smiled. "You are right," he confessed. "They're coming from me. But my calculations went wrong."

Tomsson Black told them about his plan, which he called "Plan B," for "Black." His plan was to arm all American black males, instruct them in guerilla warfare, and have them wait until he gave the order to begin waging war against the whites.

He had acquired ten million guns and a billion rounds of ammunition, and once they had all been distributed and blacks had become familiar with their use and in the tactics of guerilla warfare, he had intended to issue an ultimatum to the white race: grant us equality or kill us as a race. He planned to demonstrate to the whites that blacks were well-armed and well-trained. However, only a small percentage of the guns had been distributed and their owners were running amok with them.

"I was a fool not to have anticipated it," he confessed. Why should black men act any different from white men in a similar situation? Did black men value their lives any more than white men? Did black men value freedom any less? What was the difference between a black man and a white man whose antecedants had lived under the same society and with the same values and beliefs for three and a half centuries? Did the black man have hereditary slave compulsions passed down from one generation to another?

Tomsson Black would have liked to have had the time to organize the black race into effective guerilla units, and the units into an effective force, in order to add weight to his ultimatum. He would also have liked to have granted white people the time for reflection and consideration before they made their choice. Somehow it had gotten out of his control. Now all he could do was complete the distribution of the guns and let maniacal, unorganized, and uncontrolled blacks massacre enough whites to make a dent in the white man's hypocrisy, before the entire black race was massacred in retaliation.

In the end, it would all depend on the white man's image of himself. Could the white man reconcile the destruction of the black race with his own image as a just, civilized, and compassionate human? Was he capable of slaughtering twenty million blacks and then continue to live with himself and enjoy his own society? It had been done before. It was a calculated risk to assume that it could never happen again.

But it was a calculated risk that the black man had to take. There was no longer any point in petitioning through the white man's legal apparatus, appealing to the white man's sense of justice, morality, religion, or compassion. Black men had done this before, they were still doing it. But so far, none of the tactics tried had made a dent in the white man's impenetrable hypocrisy.

"One thing I'll tell you," Tomsson Black said. "You'd be surprised at the number of responsible white men who can be bought by a nigger whom they hate. I never tried to keep anything a secret; I just pay, like the white man does."

"Black, you're a dangerous man," Coffin Ed said.

"Dangerous for whitey," Black said, "but not for you."

"Maybe after you get all the black people killed here you can go and live in Never-Never land, but I got to live here with the white man," Coffin Ed said. "And all my family and friends got to live here. And you're gonna get us killed."

"Not necessarily," Tomsson Black said. "It's a calculated risk, as I said. The white man may be amenable."

"But I ain't gonna let you take that risk." Coffin Ed drew his long, shiny pistol. "I'm gonna kill you."

Without warning, Grave Digger drew his own revolver and shot Coffin Ed through his right hand.

"Why'd you shoot me, Digger?" Coffin Ed asked, holding his wounded hand.

"You can't kill, Black, man," Grave Digger explained. "He might be our last chance, despite the risk. I'd rather be dead than a subhuman in this world."

"And all your relatives and friends and the rest of the black people killed in the process," Coffin Ed said, chagrined.

"If that's the way the cat jumps," Digger replied.

"I don't see it that way," Coffin Ed said, reaching for his pistol with his left hand. "I'm gonna kill him so my people can live."

"Don't touch that pistol, Ed," Grave Digger warned. "Don't make me kill you, partner."

"If you try to save this maniac's life, you're gonna have to kill me, Digger."

Grave Digger let his gun answer. He shot Coffin Ed through the head. As he stood over the body of his dead friend, Tomsson Black drew a small automatic from a side table drawer and shot Grave Digger through the back of the head.

The beautiful black woman who had brought the two detectives to the house came quickly into the room and found Tomsson Black still holding the automatic in his hand. Evidently she had been evesdropping.

"But why did you kill this one," she said, lifting her hand in the direction of Grave Digger's body. "He was on your side."

"The risk was insupportable. He knew too much and he had killed his partner," Tomsson Black answered. "Whitey would make him talk if they had to take him apart, nerve by nerve."

She looked at Tomsson Black. "I hope you know what you're doing," she said.

CHESTER HIMES was born in Jefferson City, Missouri in 1909. After studying briefly at Ohio State University, he was sent to prison in 1928 for the crime of armed robbery. During his prison term, he began writing stories for black magazines and newspapers and eventually for *Esquire*. Released for good behavior in 1936, he worked at a variety of jobs while continuing to write. His first breakthrough came in 1945 with the publication of his first book, *If He Hollers Let Him Go*. He wrote four more novels, *Lonely Crusade, Cast the First Stone, The Third Generation,* and *The Primitive* before leaving the United States to live in Paris in 1953. A chance meeting with Marcel Duhamel, the editor of Editions Gallimard's *Série Noire* led Himes to begin writing detective novels that were published to wide acclaim in Paris and the rest of Europe and eventually in the United States. The first in the series, *For Love of Imabelle,* was awarded the prestigious *Grand prix de la littérature policiere,* the first such award to a non-French writer. He wrote eight more crime novels and published a satirical novel, *Pinktoes,* an experimental novel, *A Case of Rape,* several story collections, and two volumes of autobiography before debilitating illnesses claimed him at his home in Spain in 1984.

ACP-4620   2/15/94

PS
3515
I713
P58
1993

Middlebury College

0 00 02 0585258 5